8: LEAH IN TROUBLE

Ann Bryant

Pour mes très chers amis,
René et Paulette

Scholastic Children's Books,
Commonwealth House, 1–19 New Oxford Street,
London WC1A 1NU, UK
a division of Scholastic Ltd
London ~ New York ~ Toronto ~ Sydney ~ Auckland

First published by Scholastic Ltd, 1997

ISBN 0 590 13759 X

Typeset by TW Typesetting, Midsomer Norton, Avon

Printed by Cox & Wyman Ltd, Reading, Berks.

10 9 8 7 6 5 4 3 2 1

Chapter 1

Hi. I'm Leah Bryan and I'm thirteen years old. My friends call me Leah the musician because I play the violin and the piano and I love them both.

There are six of us in our group of girls who go round together. We're all thirteen and we're all in year eight at Cableden Comp. The other thing that we have in common is that we all take turns to work two hours a day (or four on a Saturday) in *The Café* in Cableden High Street. We work on a rota basis so that everyone gets a chance to do a Saturday.

I get a lovely feeling when I tell people I work in a café. It seems so grown up. The manageress of the café is called Jan Geeson. She's the aunt of one of my friends, which is how us lot all got involved in the café in the first place.

My best friend is called Andy. Her real name is

Agnès Sorrell. You see, her mum is French and her dad is English so Andy's half French. You pronounce Agnès, Ann-yes, by the way. Andy and I don't look at all alike. She's very small and dark with short dark hair, and I'm medium height with very long straight blonde hair.

We call Andy the daring one because nothing seems to faze her, well nothing except her dad. Her dad has his soft moments of course, but most of the time he's very strict. I worry about going to Andy's house when he's around, because with his hooded eyelids and dark expression, he even looks scary. Mind you, I *do* worry about most things, so I suppose this is nothing different. Andy once said that she reckoned that if I didn't have anything at all to worry about, I'd worry about that! Getting back to Andy's dad, he spends most of his time in France where he works, so I don't see him very often at all. In fact even Andy doesn't see him very often.

Fenella Brooks, or Fen, is the ambitious one and she's responsible for starting the café club. Jan Geeson, the manageress, is Fen's aunt. Fen is very slim with light brown shoulder-length hair and freckles.

Her best friend is Natasha Johnston or Tash for short. Tash is the peacemaker. She's a really kind, sweet person, and probably the second biggest worrier after me. Tash has got thick dark hair that's quite short, and dark eyes.

Then there's Luce, short for Lucy Edmunson, the crazy one, and I mean *crazy*. Luce has got a mass of blondey auburn hair and a wicked smile. She's the trendiest of us all, or at least the most fashion conscious!

Luce's best friend is called Jaimini Riva. You pronounce Jaimini, Jay-m-nee, and she's the brainy one. So you can see that Jaimini and Luce are like chalk and cheese. They're also like chalk and cheese to look at. Jaimini's got really dark skin because her mother is white and her father is black. She's got long, straight black hair and the darkest, shiniest eyes you've ever seen. I'd love to look like Jaimini.

I said I'm always worrying about something and it's true. Even right now. It's Saturday lunch-time and I'm sitting here in my room with a letter in front of me – a letter that I've read at least twenty times. It's from my friend Oliver. Well, actually he's my boyfriend except that I hardly ever see him.

Oliver's family are all friends of our family, and until our last meeting I never used to look forward to our family get-togethers, which happened about every three or four months. You see, the problem was that Oliver was so studious and boring and generally uncool. But then this amazing transformation happened, and the next time I saw him, which was at a music festival, he was totally trendy and fantastically good-looking. I suddenly found myself feeling very differently towards this new Oliver from how I'd felt towards the old one.

We've been phoning and writing to each other quite regularly ever since. At one point his family were going to move to Cableden, which would have been mega-wonderful for Oliver and me, but unfortunately they ended up moving even further away from Cableden than they were before.

I'm dying to see Oliver again and I'd really like to see him at Ryston, where he lives, rather than at Cableden. I know it's totally stupid, but I feel as though I've only just got him as a boyfriend and I'm afraid he'll take one look at Jaimini and prefer her to me. Oliver and I were once watching television together and there was a girl on this programme who looked just like Jaimini and Oliver said, "She's nice looking, isn't she?" Of course, I answered very brightly that I thought she was really lovely looking, but inside I felt worried. I can't help it.

Anyway, to get back to Oliver's letter... He wrote quite a bit of ordinary newsy stuff about school, music, his family etc., then he said...

I know a really great way you could raise extra money so you could afford the train fare to come to

Ryston one weekend – and that's by busking. Busking is really brilliant, Leah. I've been doing it on the sax recently. It was my seventeen-year-old cousin who got me started. He's earned tons of money at it. In London there are loads of buskers in the Underground. They play their instruments and leave their case open for people to chuck money in it. Of course not everybody does, but on a good day you could make pounds. I've got enough money to buy the sound system that I wanted now, so next I'm going to save up for my own sax. The sax I play at the moment belongs to my friend's sister, and she'll be wanting it back soon. Anyway, I was thinking, why don't you try busking in the café? I'm sure the manageress – what's her name? – Jan, wouldn't mind. After all, it'll probably attract more people to the café. Let me know how you get on. Look forward to your next letter. Say hello to all your friends.
Missing you loads,
Love, Oliver.

Well, it's obvious why I'm worrying, isn't it? Oliver doesn't seem very bothered about coming to Cableden to see me. I know I said I'd prefer to go to Ryston, but nevertheless I wanted Oliver to *want* to come to Cableden, and yet all he's saving up for is a new sax now he's got his sound system. Something kept telling me his priorities were not quite all they should have been. I thought that if

I read his letter yet again I'd find some little clue that he was as keen to see me as I was to see him, but it was no good, I was just getting myself into a state.

In the end I put the letter away in my secret lockable box and got ready to go out to the café. It was Andy's turn to work but the rest of us were just meeting there for a chat and a drink. The first person I met on walking through the door was Jan. In fact I nearly bumped right into her.

"Hello, Leah," she said with a tired smile. "How are you, pet? All right?"

Jan is a very kind and fair person. She's quite strict, but we all really rate her. She moves around the café very quickly and nimbly, although I must say that today she didn't look quite so speedy as usual.

Luce was the only one of the others who had arrived apart from Andy, who gave me a quick wave from the counter where she was doing milk shakes. Becky was serving at one of the tables. Becky is in her early twenties, I guess. She's very nice, although none of us feel as though we know her that well. She likes us all, but I think she prefers the company of older people. She probably finds us lot rather frivolous.

"Guess what?" Luce said with twinkling eyes, as she yanked me down into the seat next to her in true Luce fashion.

"What?" I asked dutifully.

"I've bought Jaimini the most lovely present."

"Present? Oh, present! Oh, help!" I gabbled.

I'd completely forgotten about Jaimini's brilliant achievement coming second in a national science competition. That was the main reason we were all meeting at the café, because we wanted to surprise her with some presents. She hadn't said anything, but we all knew she was disappointed not to have won the competition, because her teachers had led her to believe that she was going to, so when she didn't the disappointment was greater. I reached for my purse and undid it, knowing full well that I would find one pound eighty pence.

"Oh Luce, I'd completely forgotten. What am I going to do? She'll be here in a minute."

"How much do you want?" Luce immediately offered in her typically impulsive way.

"You're such a gem. Could you lend me three pounds until next week?"

"Yeah, course." She had the money in my hand before I could even thank her properly, so I quickly nipped off to the jeweller's, which was next door. When I got back with the most beautiful pair of moon-shaped silver earrings under five minutes later, the others were all there, but they'd delayed the present-opening ceremony until I arrived.

"Food and drink first," said Luce, taking charge. "I don't know about you but I'm starving."

Jaimini reached into her pocket.

"No, no, this one is on us," Luce went on, sounding twice her age. "We wouldn't dream of letting you pay for yourself on this great occasion!"

Oh dear! This meant I had to borrow even more money. I turned to Tash when no one was paying any attention to us and whispered, "Can you lend me a bit of money?"

She nodded and a moment later passed a five-pound note under the table. Tash is very rich, I thought, but then I remembered that she'd worked at the café the previous day. Also, Tash was good at saving money.

Jaimini was delighted with all her presents, especially the lovely lockable diary that Luce had got her. We're into lockable things at the moment and this was a particularly beautiful one with a cover that was part material. My earrings went down very well too, but I did feel a little guilty because I hadn't made very much effort, just popping next door more or less. Worse still, I'd forgotten in the first place.

As we sat there my guilt gradually grew because I remembered it was my dad's birthday in under a fortnight and it was Oliver's a week later. He was going to be fourteen. The others were all chatting and laughing happily. Even Andy had stopped work to join in the present-opening ceremony, but I found myself going more and more into myself as I worried about how I was going to be able to raise enough money to visit Oliver, wearing something nice that I would have to buy, and give him a nice present, and also get Dad a present, as well as pay back Tash the five pounds and Luce the three pounds.

"Wake up, Leah!"

"What? Oh, sorry, I was miles away."

"Yes, we know," Luce went on. "We've been trying to attract your attention for about a year!"

"Slight exaggeration," Jaimini corrected her friend, pretending to look stern.

"Sorry, I was just worrying about..."

"Oh Leah, tell us something new," Fen interrupted. "Whatever are you worrying about this time?"

I couldn't answer straight away because Andy came back and took our orders, but Luce stopped her from going and said, "We're just about to hear what Leah's latest worry is, Andy."

"Oh, it's OK, it's nothing," I quickly said.

"Tell me when I come back," said Andy. "I don't want to get behind. For some reason it seems harder work than usual today, and I'm not sure why, because there aren't that many customers."

When she'd whizzed off with her notepad I told the others how I needed to raise quite a bit of money in a hurry. They all looked sympathetic, of course, and Tash typically offered to let me do her next turn working, so I could earn more. Than Jaimini said I shouldn't have bought her the earrings, so that made me feel terrible, because I'd forgotten about that when I'd gone on about my money situation.

"I wish I dared to do what Oliver does," I said hesitantly.

"What's that?" asked Andy, eyes gleaming as she served us our drinks.

"Busking."

"Busking! Brilliant!" breathed Luce. "You could busk right here in the café," she went on excitedly. "You could entertain all those bored people with your magic touch on the violin."

"I'm sure that would really thrill them," I said sarcastically.

"Of course it would," Fen and Andy immediately attacked me. "You're so good on the violin, Leah. You could really do well in here."

"I'll do a survey and find out," offered Luce, swinging round in her chair to face a couple of women at the next table.

" 'Scuse me," she launched in, in her usual act-now-think-later fashion, "I'm doing a survey on entertainment," she continued gravely. "Would you mind answering one simple question for me?"

The women looked at each other as though rather confused. I wasn't surprised. Luce could confuse the most calm, collected person.

"Er, what's the question then?" asked one of them.

"Do you think this café would benefit from a bit of live music?"

Again the women looked at each other. It was obvious they didn't really care either way. "Um, yes, I suppose it would be quite nice," one of them finally said.

"Thank you," said Luce, flashing them a big smile before spinning back to us with a triumphant look on her face. "See?" she said.

"Yes, they sounded very convincing," I said, even more sarcastically.

"No, but seriously, Leah, I think you ought to try it," Jaimini said. And Tash was nodding gravely. As Jaimini and Tash are probably the most sensible of us all, I did actually stop and think that maybe, just maybe, it was a possibility.

"Ask Jan," Luce commanded.

"I shouldn't," Andy said carefully, which made us all turn our attention instantly to her. "I don't know what's the matter with Jan. She's very snappy for no real reason and she's moving much more slowly than usual."

Fen immediately looked concerned and when Jan went past our table a moment later, we all asked her if she was all right.

"Just a bit tired. I'll be OK," she said, with a weary smile.

Andy was right. It wouldn't be a good moment to talk about busking. I'd leave it till Monday.

About half an hour later we were on the point of leaving the café when Andy came over looking really alarmed.

"Can you come into the kitchen a minute, Fen? Becky's gone a bit early and Kevin went a little while ago, so there's only me here and Jan doesn't seem at all well."

Kevin is the chef, by the way. He's twenty-one and really good-looking. He's also a very nice guy, kind, sensitive and a man of very few words.

We waited anxiously until Fen reappeared.

"I think one of us ought to stay to help," she said. "Jan's obviously sickening for something. She's really tired and just not herself."

"I'll stay," I immediately volunteered.

"I don't think it'll be paid," Fen said.

"No, that's OK," I quickly assured her.

So Fen and I stayed together with Andy. We kept Jan in the kitchen and gave her a cup of tea. She smiled gratefully when we told her there were no arguments, we were simply taking over until six-thirty. On Saturdays the café closes at six and the last half-hour is just cleaning and clearing, so as soon as six o'clock came and the CLOSED sign was safely in place, we told Jan to go home, and assured her that we would do the lock-up. Although Jan insisted that she was all right to drive herself home, Fen phoned her mum and Dee turned up to collect Jan.

It was a quarter to seven when I got home and Mum wasn't too happy because I hadn't phoned and she was expecting me back earlier. I explained about Jan, which pacified her slightly, then I went upstairs and took out my violin.

I'd hardly looked at it before Kim came in and plonked herself on my bed. Kim is my fifteen-year-old sister. People say she looks like me, but actually there's one big difference. Kim has got some kind of magnetic ingredient in her looks because she attracts boys without even trying. She's very natural, wears little or no make-up, and has her hair loose all the time. Her hair is darker and thicker than mine but just as long. Despite all that, I'm not jealous of her. She's a lovely big sister and we're very close.

People think we're a very close family altogether, but we're not particularly. Mum and Dad are close to each other even though they're not at all alike, and Kim and I, as I said, are also very fond of each other.

Dad is a sweet old-fashioned man who often

smokes a pipe. My friends are all fascinated by Dad and his pipe. Mum is more brisk and organized and comes from a very poor background. She's determined that Kim and I will do well in life, that's why she and Dad stretch themselves to pay for my music lessons. They don't have to pay for Kim any more because she's given up her music, which broke Mum and Dad's hearts. Although Dad is very laid back about me and my music, Mum pushes me to get better and better. She's very proud of me, but sometimes it gets really embarrassing when she wants me to play for visitors.

Mum works really hard. She works for an estate agency, but she doesn't get paid very much and has to work quite long hours. Dad works for someone who owns a small business buying and selling stamps. When Dad was a boy, he and all his friends used to collect stamps, but boys don't do that very much these days, so there's quite a risk that Dad could be made redundant. For the moment things are OK, and he always tries to give the impression that he's not worrying about the future, but I've heard him talking to Mum, and I can tell he is.

"You're not practising now, surely?" said Kim.

"No, just looking," I answered, which made us both splutter out a giggle because it was such a silly reply.

"Kim…?"

She waited.

"Have you ever busked?"

"No."

"I'm thinking of busking in the café."

Her eyes widened. I could tell she was impressed. "In the café? Does Jan mind?"

"I've not asked her yet."

"But why busking anyway?"

"Because I need the money."

"You must need it really badly if you're thinking of busking. I didn't think you'd have the guts to stand up and play your violin in front of lots of people who are just minding their own business, eating, drinking and talking."

I shivered at this thought. I'd suddenly had such a clear picture of what it would be like.

"No, you're right. I hope Jan says, 'No, you can't, Leah.'"

Again we both cracked up because I'd just said such a ridiculous thing. After all, if I didn't want to busk there was no need to ask Jan, was there?

"Look, shall I just lend you some money?" Kim asked. "I've not got much but I could manage a fiver."

"I need more than that. It's my own fault for spending my money on that concert ticket."

"Well, yes, I did think that was a bit rash."

I had been desperate to see Oliver and he had

been going to a Classical Spectacular evening. The venue for the concert was roughly halfway between Ryston and Cableden, so I'd gone on the train and his mum and dad picked me up, then we'd all gone to the concert together. I'd used up all the money I'd saved.

"So what do you need the money for this time?" Kim asked.

I felt slightly embarrassed to admit it was to see Oliver again. I knew Kim would jump down my throat, and she did.

"Why can't he come and see *you*?" she asked indignantly. "You mustn't do all the running, you know," she added.

"Well, he could come and see me but I'd rather go to Ryston. I've never been there. Anyway, last time I didn't do all the running. We met halfway," I defended myself.

"Hm," she answered, unconvinced.

"Anyway, it's not just to see Oliver that I need the money. It's for Dad's birthday ... and Oliver's birthday," I trailed off.

After a brief, thoughtful silence, Kim suddenly jumped up and gave me a hug. "If that's what you want, you ought to go for it," she said. "It'll do you good, you know, busking at the café. It'll strengthen your character."

I felt heartened by her sudden positiveness.

"I'll speak to Jan on Monday," I told her.

"You'll be great, Lee, I know it," she went on enthusiastically.

I smiled at her. She was so encouraging and confident about me.

Unfortunately I never did get to ask Jan about it on Monday, because just then the phone rang. Mum answered it and called up to me that it was Fen, so I whizzed downstairs.

"Hi, Fen!"

"Something terrible's happened."

"What? What!"

"Jan's collapsed. She's being taken to hospital by Mum. We don't know what's the matter with her yet. Mum's just phoned from Jan's to say she'll be late."

"Omigod!"

"I know."

"Oh, poor Jan!"

"I know."

"Have you told the others?"

"Only Tash so far."

"I'll tell Andy."

"Yeah, thanks."

"Bye, Fen! Speak to you tomorrow."

"Bye."

I sat down heavily in the nearest chair and thought back to Jan's tired face and slow movement in the café. Poor, poor Jan.

Chapter 2

On Sunday morning the six of us all got together at Fen's place, and Fen's mum, Dee, tried to answer all the questions we bombarded her with, although it was almost impossible for her.

"She's got raised blood pressure, and she's likely to be in hospital for about a week. They want to do various tests to check it's nothing more than that. Poor Jan has been overdoing it for far too long and this, unfortunately, is the result. She'll need a few days to recover at home too, before she'll be fit enough to come back to the café."

Much more than that Dee couldn't really tell us. The thing that we were all dying to know was what was going to happen to the café, but none of us wanted to ask too soon in case it sounded as though we only cared about our jobs and weren't really interested in Jan's health.

"Did Jan say anything about the café, Mum?" Fen finally asked.

"Yes, she did," answered Dee, reaching for her shoulder bag and rooting around inside it. "Here we are," she said, producing a neatly folded piece of paper. "Hilda Salmon."

"Who's Hilda Salmon?" asked Fen.

"She's that neighbour of Jan's... You know – Jan's mentioned her quite a few times. Well, that's who Jan wants to take over while she's away."

"Oh," said Fen, looking as surprised as I felt.

"Apparently Jan was thinking of having two weeks off in a few months' time, and she'd already sounded out this Hilda Salmon to take over for that period. So all that's happened is that the fortnight has been brought forward, unfortunately for Jan."

"So why Hilda Salmon?" asked Luce, wrinkling her nose.

"Because she used to manage a small café in London a few years back, and apparently she told Jan some time ago that if ever she wanted a break, she'd be happy to step in."

Luce was still wrinkling her nose, but now she'd started shaking her head as well, as though she thought the choice of Hilda Salmon was really a bad one.

"Did you think Jan would have chosen you, Luce?" asked Jaimini with a wicked grin.

"Course not!" Luce replied hotly. "I thought Debra actually."

"So did I," Tash and I admitted at the same time.

"Well, I think it's because Debra didn't want to work full time," explained Dee. "Anyway, it's all settled and Jan particularly wanted me to tell you that until she gets back, Hilda Salmon is in charge, and if you have any problems you take them to her. Jan's very sensibly decided to hand over the total responsibility of the café, so that she can concentrate on getting better as quickly as possible. If she starts worrying about things while she's in hospital it'll take all the longer for her to get better. Incidentally, I got the impression that Hilda might not run things in exactly the same way as Jan does, but that doesn't mean that you should treat her with any less respect than you do Jan. All right?"

We all nodded gravely then went up to Fen's room and sat round on the floor in a circle. We played a game of guessing what Hilda Salmon would look like, how old she'd be and how nice she'd be. We finally settled on very nice, late forties, tall and thin with short, dark, permed hair.

The other thing that we settled on was that, once we were sure she was allowed to make big decisions about the café, we'd ask her whether she would give permission for me to try busking.

A little thread of guilt was weaving itself into my mind because deep down I knew that Jan would never have said yes to me busking, so I would be deliberately using her unfortunate illness to my own advantage. The others were getting really excited at the thought of it, but I just felt scared, which may well have been because of the guilt.

On Monday we couldn't get through school fast enough to get down to the café. It was my turn to work and I'd half expected Hilda Salmon to phone me on Sunday, just to introduce herself and confirm that I would be there, but there'd been no phone call.

One thing I had done on Sunday, though, was to write to Oliver. I'd actually told him that I was going to ask permission to busk in the café, and I'd also posted the letter so now I *had* to ask, otherwise Oliver might think I was wimpish, and of course I only wanted to be perfect in Oliver's eyes.

I'd also told him in my letter that I was saving up to go and visit him, then I'd talked about Jan and the café and school and friends. I hoped I wouldn't have to wait too long for a reply. Oliver wasn't quite as good as I was about keeping our communication up. I'd never let that bother me, because I knew that boys in general were less communicative than girls.

At five o'clock I went nervously through the

back door of the café into the kitchen. The others all went in through the main café door. For some reason or other I was expecting the kitchen to look different as Jan wouldn't be there, so it came as quite a shock to find it looking exactly the same as usual, except for a piece of paper with all our names and phone numbers on it Sellotaped to the wall.

"Hello, Leah," Kevin said with a smile. "How's things?"

"Fine, thanks. What about the café? What's it like without Jan?"

Kevin's eyes didn't leave the top of his Aga on which there were various pans on the go.

"All right," he told me briefly. Why did I get the feeling that he didn't exactly mean that?

I reached for a clean white apron as the door opened. It was Becky. Her lips were pursed. She didn't see me at first.

"Silly old bag," she said under her breath to no one in particular, but I've got very good hearing and so has Kevin. We both stopped what we were doing and looked at Becky.

"Oh, Leah, hi. I didn't know you'd arrived," she said, glancing up and looking a bit flustered.

"Evidently not," said Kevin, giving me a quick wink, which showed he knew I'd heard what Becky had said.

"What's she like?" I asked Becky in a whisper,

just in case Hilda Salmon suddenly came into the kitchen.

"Not my cup of tea, I'm afraid," Becky replied, pursing her lips again and throwing herself back into her work as if to show that that was the end of the conversation.

I realized I'd just have to see for myself so I went into the café to ask Hilda Salmon what she wanted me to do. Normally I would just get on with something, but I thought I ought to at least introduce myself and get off to a good start. After all, I needed her on my side for when I got the courage to ask about the busking.

The moment I entered the café I sensed a change in the atmosphere. Even if I'd been blind, and no one had told me that Jan wasn't there, I think I would have known instantly that something was different.

We were completely wrong about Hilda Salmon. She was medium height and rather – no, make that *very* – plump, with a reddish face. She was sweating slightly and her eyes were darting about all over the place. Her hair was blonde with dark roots. I know you shouldn't judge people on their appearance but I couldn't help it, so my first reaction to Hilda Salmon was that I didn't really like her. As soon as that thought had entered my head I pushed it out and told myself off. "Stop being so unfair, Leah. The poor woman has taken over with scarcely any notice. She can't help it if she's not had time to get her roots done."

I glanced at the others and Andy lifted one side of her lip in a grimace that she'd perfected. I grinned, then quickly turned it into what I hoped was a welcoming smile because I realized that I was being approached by the new manageress.

"Leah Bryan?" she asked. Her tone wasn't particularly welcoming but then it wasn't particularly unwelcoming either.

I nodded and kept up the smile, then asked in my politest voice, "I wondered what you'd like me to start with?"

She gave me a look which said, "Well, if you don't know what to do without me telling you every time, we're not going to get very far." What she actually said though was, "No need to ask me every time. Just keep your eyes open and do whatever needs doing. That's the way I operate so that's the way it's going to be all the time I'm here."

If I'd been Andy I might have been tempted to tell her that actually I was perfectly capable of working out for myself what needed doing, but I had thought it only polite to check first that that was the way she wanted things run. But I'm not Andy so I just stood there looking pathetic, then scuttled off mumbling about washing-up when her expression didn't alter after about five seconds.

"See what you mean," I said quietly to Becky as I passed her in the doorway. And for the first time ever, I didn't particularly enjoy my work that day. I managed to get a quick conversation with the others when Hilda was in the kitchen.

"Isn't she awful!" Luce immediately began.

"Awful," I agreed.

"It's going to seem weird calling her Hilda," Andy commented.

"Well, we could say Mrs Salmon, I suppose," suggested Jaimini.

"No, that would be too much like school," Fen said.

"Fancy having to put up with *that* for the next fortnight," Luce said aggressively.

Tash smiled a sympathetic smile as she said, "I suppose the busking idea is out of the question, Leah?"

I nodded.

"No, it's not," Andy said in her usual soft, decisive way. We all looked at her, waiting for her to go on.

"We're not going to let her boss us around, are we," she said, her eyes glinting challengingly.

"Well..." I began.

"It wasn't a question," she interrupted. "Go for it, Lee. Throw your weight around a bit. I'm going to when it's my turn."

"That's not till Friday," I pointed out.

"You can have my turn tomorrow if you want," Fen said, looking thoroughly fed up.

"Yes, OK, I will," Andy replied, sitting up straight.

"You're mad," I informed her half jokingly.

"Whoops! Here she comes," Tash said, looking guilty. Without another word I turned and marched back to the kitchen. I didn't look in Hilda's direction so I wouldn't know whether she was glaring at me, but it certainly felt as though she was.

In the kitchen, Becky was complaining to Kevin about "that awful woman". Kevin wasn't paying any attention, just listening as usual. Becky looked close to tears.

"Who does she think she is, bossing us about, Kevin? I've been here ages and she treats me like I only started today."

"Don't let her get to you," Kevin advised calmly. "It's not worth it – she's only here for a short while."

"I can't help letting her get to me. She's already got to me so it's too late," Becky moaned.

"No, it's not. Just put up with her for two weeks, then you never need set eyes on her again."

"What do *you* think of her, Leah?" Becky asked.

I felt quite flattered that Becky was interested in my opinion.

"I don't really like her," I said, biting my lip.

"There's no need to look apologetic," Becky said, getting excited again; then the door opened so she abruptly clammed up, and stormed out of the kitchen, almost knocking Hilda off balance as she brushed past her ferociously.

"Well!" uttered Hilda as though such behaviour was totally beyond her comprehension.

Kevin carried on cooking without reacting and I started putting things away as though I hadn't noticed that she'd even come in.

At five-twenty-five, Hilda announced that I could start hoovering the café.

"But it's not half past yet," I pointed out, glancing at my watch.

"And there's next to no one in the café," she replied slowly as though I was thick.

I went in to find two ladies chatting and finishing their coffees. I couldn't possibly start hoovering while there were still customers in the café. Jan had always been very strict about consideration to the customer, and it was just as though Hilda was the complete opposite. I decided I'd busy myself watering the plants and wiping the counter, both jobs which also needed doing, but weren't so intrusive.

"Could have sworn I said to do the hoovering," came the dreaded voice as Hilda came puffing up behind me. She always seemed out of breath. I was sure she was carrying too much weight around with her and that was why she perspired so much.

"I was waiting for those two ladies to go," I whispered.

For answer she turned on her heel and came back with the vacuum cleaner, which she dumped in the middle of the café and plugged in at the wall. Then she disappeared back into the kitchen. This was like the broadest hint in the world for me to get vacuuming and also for the two ladies to get going. I felt very embarrassed and when the two women started gulping their drinks, leaning forwards with their shoulders raised, I glanced behind me to check that Hilda hadn't returned, then I told the women to take as long as they wanted.

The next time Hilda appeared, she looked pointedly at her watch (it was twenty-five to six), and then with an impatient gesture she took hold of the vacuum and began dragging it violently around herself. I wished at that moment that I could explain to the two women that this manageress was only a stand-in, and that the regular one, who was much nicer, would be back soon. It suddenly seemed blatantly clear to me that the café was going to go downhill rapidly if Hilda Salmon carried on like this. Something would have to be done.

Maybe whoever was on duty the following day ought to have a word with Becky and Kevin, and see if either or both of them would speak to Hilda and point out to her that she'd better ease up a bit if she wanted to keep any customers at all.

As I was thinking this, I could hear Dee's voice in the back of my mind... *Jan particularly wanted me to tell you that until she gets back, Hilda Salmon is in charge... Jan's decided to hand over the total responsibility of the café... Hilda might not run things in quite the same way, but you must accept whatever she does and treat her with the same respect as you give Jan...* Still, it would be Andy on duty the next day because she had taken Fen's place, and what better one out of us all to cope with Hilda?

That evening I spent ages on the phone giving Andy a blow by blow account of just how bad Hilda Salmon was. The following day at school we discussed it with the others and of course we all wound each other up, so that by the end of school when the bell rang, Andy was prepared for battle as she grabbed her bag and made for the main exit. The rest of us followed behind, literally.

It's always absolutely clear when Andy is feeling positive about something, because she moves about twice as fast as anyone else. You might call it purposeful, except that purposeful isn't purposeful enough for Andy!

We all struggled to keep up with her. In the end, Tash and I gave up. Jaimini and Luce were a little ahead of us. Fen was the only one who was almost managing to keep up. So by the time Tash and I went into the café the others had got the table and even ordered the drinks.

Mark was on duty instead of Becky. Becky, Mark and Debra are the other three part-timers at the café. Becky or Mark is always on with one of us and they also do lunchtimes. Debra arrives at nine in the morning and leaves at three, so we never see her because she doesn't do Saturdays at all. We'd all wondered how Debra had coped with Hilda Salmon, but short of ringing her up and asking her, we'd never know.

Mark is seventeen. He looks very strong and fit. He's studying martial arts at the moment, which is his big passion. He probably won't be at the café much longer. He just works there to make a bit of extra money and he also coaches judo in the evenings.

"What's this gathering in aid of?" he asked, as Tash and I sat down. "Sizing up the new management, are we, girls?" Mark grinned at us.

"What do *you* think of her?" I asked him.

"I think I'll keep my head down for the next two weeks, otherwise she'll get to me like she has to Becky."

"I know," I said, remembering Becky moaning

in the kitchen to Kevin. "She was really fed up yesterday."

"And today she's gone," Mark finished off.

"What!" we all gasped.

"Gone. Had enough," he said with a shrug. "You know Becky. She won't put up with any nonsense. She said she wasn't going to set foot in this place until Jan got back, even if that *did* mean forgoing her wages for a couple of weeks."

"Jan might want to know about this," Fen said thoughtfully when Mark had gone to get our drinks.

"Perhaps she *does* know," Jaimini said.

"Don't forget what Dee said, though," Tash reminded us. "Jan doesn't want to know – not at the moment. It'll make her worse." Tash's tone changed. "Uh-oh, here comes the dragon."

"She's coming over here!" squeaked Luce. "It wasn't me, miss, honestly!" she added in a silly, high-pitched voice, putting a napkin over her head. Luce really could play the fool at the most inappropriate times. The rest of us just ignored her, though it was hard not to crack up. Hilda Salmon was standing by my chair. I prayed that she hadn't realized that Luce was taking the mickey out of her.

"Andrea said you wanted to ask me something," she said, without wasting any time on hellos or how-are-yous.

I frowned, and then, as I realized who Andrea was and what she meant, my heart started to pound.

"It's Andy," Fen corrected Hilda.

"Hm. I don't go in for nicknames much myself."

"Well, her proper name is Agnès," Luce explained, deliberately pronouncing the name with an over-the-top French accent.

"Well, whatever it is, I gather you play the violin rather well, Leah."

I gave a very faint nod because I didn't want to give the impression that I thought I was anything special, but on the other hand I didn't want to lose this opportunity that Andy had obviously set up for me.

"She says you fancy a bit of busking," Hilda went on, and then something amazing happened. Her face actually cracked slightly and a bit of a smile appeared. It suddenly occurred to me that I'd never seen her smile before. And quite honestly, if you'd asked me to guess what I thought would make Hilda Salmon smile, the very last thing I would have guessed would have been a discussion about me busking at the café. A quick glance round the table showed me that the others were as surprised as I was.

"Leah's fantastic on the violin," Luce put in.

"Yes, she's absolutely brilliant," Tash added,

and the others all said something similar which made me start to worry because they were building me up to be really wonderful, and Hilda Salmon might not have the same idea when she heard me.

"Had a feller at the other café where I used to work years ago. He busked on the fiddle... Brought the custom in like nothing else could, he did." She was smiling but not at us; more at the memory really.

"When do you want to start?" she suddenly asked, snapping her eyes back to my face.

"Er ... when do you suggest?" I asked carefully.

"How about tomorrow?"

"Er ... yes, all right." There was something else I was worried about. "What sort of thing did the man at your old café play?"

"All sorts. Bit of gypsy, bit of folk, bit of jazz, bit of classics – marvellous!"

I gulped and was about to tell her I wasn't sure if I could manage all that, when Luce came in with, "Leah can do all those styles – you'll see."

"Actually, I'm not all that good..." I began.

"Yes, you are," Andy said, appearing from nowhere and plonking herself confidently beside Hilda. "Don't listen to her, Hilda."

As Andy said this she gave Hilda a friendly nudge as though the two of them had been good mates for years. "She's always far too modest."

"And what's this French name you've got?" Hilda changed the subject, turning to Andy in a perfectly friendly way. The rest of us couldn't believe what we were seeing. Andy had cracked it. She had somehow discovered the best way to get Hilda Salmon in a good mood.

"Oh, just call me Andy. Everyone else does."

"Oh, do they indeed?" Hilda sniffed as she slowly ambled back to work.

Andy paused for a second to give the thumbs-up sign, then followed in Hilda's wake.

"She reminds me of a puff-adder, the way she puffs about everywhere," Luce remarked conversationally.

"Yes, it looks like Andy's the little lizard following the big puff-adder," Jaimini agreed with a giggle.

"Well," said Fen as soon as they were out of earshot. "What a turn up for the books!"

"She's such a mixture, isn't she?" Tash commented.

"I quite agree," I said with feeling.

"I'm not sure I trust her," Fen added slowly.

"If Andy trusts her, I'm sure she must be all right," Luce said with a frown, as though she wasn't quite sure why Andy trusted her. I knew what she meant. It was completely out of character for Andy. She was normally the least trusting of us all.

"What's Andy up to?" Fen asked me, as though I'd be able to dip into Andy's brain and tell her the answer.

I did a "search-me" gesture, then got back to worrying about busking. "I don't think I can do it," I began hesitantly. "I mean, I don't think I've got the guts or the talent."

"You've got the talent, that's for sure," Tash assured me. "And once you've started you'll relax. It'll just be those first few notes that'll be difficult."

"But what will I *do* exactly?" I asked, feeling myself getting tense with worry, and badly regretting having ever even considered busking in the first place. If only Oliver had never mentioned it. The thought of Oliver gave me a bit of courage. He'd be proud of me. I bet he'd never dream that I'd actually dare to do it.

"All you do is start playing," Luce informed me as though it was the easiest thing in the world, and she'd do it herself if only she had a fiddle. "If I could play the violin like you, I'd be dying to show off," she added, perfectly seriously.

"Well, I'm dreading it," I said with an involuntary shiver.

"Just think of the money," Jaimini advised.

"Becky's left," Andy said in a loud stage-whisper when she next passed our table.

"So Mark said," Fen replied.

"Hilda's definitely getting to Mark as well," Andy added. "*And* Kevin – and that's a bad sign." Andy's eyes were full of mistrust and suspicion.

"I thought she was your best mate," Luce said, a bit too loudly.

"Ssh! You must be joking!" replied Andy. "I don't trust her at all. I'm just trying to fathom her. According to Mark, Debra isn't that enamoured either."

"How did you manage to introduce the topic of busking?" Fen asked.

"I didn't. *She* did. She started going on about the café where she used to be the manageress. I could tell she obviously loved it, so when she threw in that there was always live music in the café, I decided that it would be a good moment to mention Leah. The only trouble is – Kevin."

"Kevin!"

"Yes. He didn't look very approving."

"Well, Kevin won't have to listen. He's never out of the kitchen, is he?" Luce remarked reasonably.

I left the café first that day because I wanted to get home and start practising like mad. As I was practising I realized that there were tons of things I hadn't worked out, like where I would actually stand in the café, and how long I should play for, and should I leave my violin case open on the floor or what? I know most people would never dream of worrying about such details, but I'm the world's worst worrier as you know.

In the end I got myself in such a state that I phoned Andy. Her mum told me that Andy was out running. That proved that Andy hadn't enjoyed the café work. I know my best friend very well and she wasn't training for anything in particular, so the only reason she would go out for a run after working at the café was if she felt frustrated.

Next I phoned Fen. She told me that her mother had been to see Jan and that Jan was very groggy and low. Fen said that she'd asked her mum whether or not Jan had asked about the café and how it was all going, but her mum had said, "Of course not. I told you she wants a complete break from the place, so quite honestly, even if the place had burnt down I wouldn't want to trouble Jan with it until she's better."

As I lay in bed that night I thought back over that conversation and it somehow made me feel insecure. I think the truth was that in my heart of hearts I didn't really want to busk and I was kind of hoping that if Jan knew about it, and refused to give permission for me to do it, then I wouldn't have the choice.

"Think of Oliver, think of Oliver," I told myself over and over again, and that helped. I *would* do it. I'd do it for Oliver, and the money would be a bonus.

Chapter 3

The following morning I woke up to nervousness, and immediately practised my violin for half an hour. I reckoned I could play for twenty-five minutes without repeating myself but after that I'd run out of things that I knew.

"That was a good old play you were having up there," Mum said with a big smile, when we were all having breakfast.

I was tempted to tell her about the busking, but I didn't because I knew full well that she'd never approve of such a thing. Mum likes me to play in concerts and festivals and take exams, but she'd think busking didn't have quite a serious enough image, and she'd also say that I was far too young.

"This came," said Kim, dropping a letter on to my plate. She gave me a knowing smile because she'd obviously recognized Oliver's big sprawly handwriting. I don't like reading Oliver's letters in front of my family so I folded it in two and stuffed it in the pocket of my school shirt, under my jumper, to read later in private. The letter lifted my spirits a little, but still I knew I'd have trouble getting through the day at school.

At morning break the others all crowded round me, checking that I'd got my violin, encouraging me not to be nervous, assuring me that everything would be fine once I'd played the first few notes. I admired their confidence and wished a bit of it would rub off on me.

We discussed Hilda Salmon at length and all agreed that she was a peculiar mixture of strict and lax, and definitely not to be trusted.

"Did you tell your mum that Becky had left?" Jaimini asked Fen.

"No, I didn't. Something told me that it was best not to mention it. After all, what could Jan do about it while she's lying in a hospital bed?"

It wasn't until the lesson just before lunch, which was science with Mr Hawkenbury, that I remembered Oliver's letter. We were writing up conclusions to experiments that we'd just done. Some people were still actually doing the experiments, but I was back in my place. A quick glance round told me that Mr Hawkenbury had his back to me and was heavily into staring at someone's test-tube, so I pulled out Oliver's letter and put it in my lap to read.

"What you got, Leah?" asked a girl called Emma, leaning over my shoulder. She was the class busybody, always being nosey. If it had been any of the others they probably would have told her where to go, but being me I just put my hand over the letter and said, "Nothing."

"Come on, show us," she said, trying to get my hand off the letter. She was holding a little phial of some bluey liquid in her other hand, but because her attention was totally on my letter, which she obviously thought was something much more exciting than it really was, the phial tipped and splashed a few blobs of blue on to the letter and on to my hands. I watched aghast as the blue spread out on the paper.

"Now look what you've done, Emma, you clumsy thing," snapped Andy, coming back to her place beside me and taking in the situation at a glance. "You're so nosey you've messed up Leah's letter from her boyfriend."

"Oh, sorry, Leah," mumbled Emma, because she's not horrible or anything, just really nosey. Not many people in our class have got boyfriends. Although everybody talks about going out with people, it doesn't really mean much, so those who've got proper boyfriends come in for a lot of admiration, and that's why Emma was so apologetic.

"It's OK," I mumbled, glancing up to check

that old Hawk-Eye, as we call him, hadn't noticed us. He hadn't. Emma went sadly off, leaving me to read what I could of the letter. I got the impression as I was reading that Oliver hadn't received my letter when he was writing this one to me. His big news was that his mother had got a lodger to stay to try and earn some extra money.

"*Her d...*" – the next bit was covered by a blue blob – "*is really great.*"

What? I reread that bit, desperately trying to make out what was written under the blue blob, but it was impossible. "*She...*" – tons more blue – "*room when I was on my computer, and seemed fascinated by it...*" – more blue – "*the name Tara very much, but still. I took her...*" – more blobby blue – "*we both enjoyed it especially...*" – yet more – "*Anyway she'll be here for a while so it's a good job that we get on.*"

I skimmed through the rest of Oliver's letter which was about school, and then some film he'd been to see, and finally the last paragraph said he'd just got my letter and wished me luck with busking. I folded the letter up and stuffed it back into my pocket.

"What are you scowling for?" asked Andy, cutting into my thoughts.

"Oh, nothing," I answered, but I felt close to tears, and it must have been obvious to Andy, who knew me so well. She gave me a searching look and I found myself telling her about the letter.

"Oliver's mum's got this lodger," I began with a sigh, "and apparently the daughter's staying there too. She's called Tara and it sounds like Oliver thinks she's the greatest thing that ever walked God's earth."

"How old is she?"

"Dunno. He doesn't say. Only that she's fascinated by his computer and he took her out somewhere, and she's going to be around for quite a while."

Andy gasped. "Took her out!" Then her face cleared and she smiled. "I shouldn't worry about it, Leah. After all, if he's telling *you* about it, it can't be a big deal, can it? I mean if it was anything for you to worry about, Oliver would be keeping it a secret, wouldn't he?"

"Suppose so," I mumbled. I felt so depressed. I didn't take in a single thing for the whole of the rest of science, then at lunchtime I went off to the loo, sat on the lid and read the letter again.

This time it seemed even worse somehow. It was almost as though Oliver was desperate to talk about this Tara girl. In fact he was so desperate that he'd decided he'd have to mention her to *me* even! How thoughtless and insensitive of him! How dare he! I'd never be so horrible as to go on about some boy who was staying with us, then tell Oliver in a letter about how we really enjoyed going out together. The more I thought about it the angrier I got, and by the time I rejoined Andy I was really furious.

"Why don't you give him a bit of his own medicine?" Andy suggested with a wicked gleam in her eye. "See how *he* likes it!"

"What do you mean?"

"Invent a really good-looking boy who you met in the café."

I considered this for a moment and then we both clutched each other and let out a whoop of delight.

"Yes, I will!" I announced with great determination.

"You mustn't make it too obvious or he'll suss you," Andy went on, really getting into the idea. "Just drop the name in a couple of times, then expand on it in the next letter."

"Yes, that's brilliant, Andy. What shall we call him?"

"Um ... how about Pete?"

"Yes, that sounds ordinary enough. Pete it is. So what does he look like?"

"Tall, dark, devastatingly gorgeous, you know, usual stuff!"

"I can feel myself falling for him already," I laughed.

During the afternoon my brief light-headedness fizzled out and left me with the depressing truth that Tara really *did* exist, whereas Pete was simply a figment of my imagination. And to make me feel even worse, the busking was coming nearer and nearer and I was getting more and more jelly-kneed and scared stiff than ever.

We all went down to the café together and guessed on the way what kind of mood Hilda Salmon would be in. It was Luce's turn to work. When we first walked in, the place was fairly empty and I grabbed Andy's arm and told her it was no good, I couldn't possibly play because it would seem ridiculous with so few people there. I'd already told Luce to ask Hilda to let me know when she wanted me to start.

"Start whenever you want, Leah," called out Hilda casually across the café about five minutes later. All the customers turned to stare at me when she said that, and I didn't know where to put myself. Then a few more customers came in and neither Luce nor Hilda were taking any notice of me at all. They were both engrossed in their work.

I managed to attract Luce's attention and she came over, but said she couldn't stop because she was doing two people's work as neither Becky nor Mark was there, and Hilda wasn't such a quick worker as Jan.

"Shall I start playing, do you think?" I asked

Luce in a shaky whisper.

"Yeah, go for it," she answered, before dashing back to the kitchen. It was all so unimportant to Luce, so why was it such a monumental effort for me?

The next time Hilda glanced over I quickly stood up with my violin, thinking it's now or never. She gave me a sort of curt little nod and I rushed over to ask her where I should stand.

"Where you like," she answered unhelpfully. "Over there, I should say," she added, pointing towards a corner, so over I went, my heart pounding furiously. What I was praying more than ever was that no one from our school would come in – especially no teachers.

As I took out my violin I was aware that everybody was watching me, some discreetly, some quite openly, and all my friends' faces were wreathed in encouraging smiles, all except Tash, who was looking pale and concerned, but probably not half as pale and concerned as I looked.

The moment had come. I'd got my shoulder-rest in place, I'd put rosin on my bow. I knew my violin was in tune, because I'd checked at the end of school, so I tucked it up under my chin, my bowing arm poised. I saw Luce across the room stick up one finger, then two, then three, then mouth, "Go!" And I did.

My first note as a busker hit the air. It was the note D and it was probably the worst D I'd ever played in my life because my bow was wobbling violently. Still, there was nothing for it, I had to go on. I was starting with a piece called *Allegro* by Fiocco, which was fast and rhythmic. The moment I'd started I regretted the choice because it was too startling and classical-sounding. Everybody seemed to be sitting bolt upright all of a sudden.

Oh, why hadn't I asked Kim to suggest something for me to play, something nice and soothing and backgroundish? My first few bars seemed to be full of mistakes, and I didn't dare raise my eyes and look round to see how people were reacting. All I knew was that the place was totally silent apart from the sound of my violin. Surely this wasn't right? Surely people were supposed to carry on talking? My face felt as though all the blood had drained from it, and my knees really were trembling. I told myself to pull myself together and try to get through the piece without any major stumbles, then move on to something that was easy to play, but sounded really smooth and impressive.

Once I'd made this decision the end of the piece seemed to come really quickly, and as I struck the last chord, all the blood came rushing back to my face because Luce, who was standing in the middle of the café, did one of those loud whistles with two fingers in her mouth. At least that diverted the attention from me for a moment. The others clapped enthusiastically and even Hilda clapped, although she didn't smile. When the clapping had subsided she announced that if anyone wanted to show their appreciation, the violin case was the place to show it! That made me feel really embarrassed.

Hilda, on the other hand, grinned round at everyone, and because she sounded confident and relaxed, all the customers seemed to relax too. I opened my case on the table in front of me and carried on playing. This time I felt about twenty times better because people carried on talking as though I was just the background, which was precisely what I wanted to be.

After that I rolled each piece into the next one so that there wasn't a definite stopping time. I'd never realized how tiring it was to play continually like this in a public place. I'd often practised at home for up to an hour and a half, but somehow that wasn't as exhausting as this.

The most thrilling moment came when four women got up to go and as they went out, they each dropped a few coins into my case. When I smiled at them, they all smiled back and one of them mouthed "Very good" to me. As I carried on playing I tried to inch forwards a bit so that I could see what coins they'd put in. Hilda wasn't as subtle as me. The moment the women had gone she went straight up to the table where the case was, and craned her neck to look in it, while pretending to be on her way to take down a poster from the wall just behind me.

Andy rolled her eyes at me, and I returned a more subtle version of the same look. The others mimed a brief spurt of clapping to show me that they thought it was going well, and I began to feel better and better because two more customers put money into the case over the next few minutes.

The only thing that was making me anxious was that a tall man had walked into the café a couple of minutes before, and he hadn't taken his eyes off me the whole time I was playing. I knew that because every time I looked up our eyes met, which began to make me very hot and bothered.

I glanced at the café clock and realized that I'd been playing for nearly half an hour, and I was absolutely exhausted, so I lowered my bow and was about to put my violin in the case when Hilda appeared in front of me.

"What are you doing?" she hissed, in a not very subtle stage-whisper.

"I thought I'd just have a break. I'm really … tired, you see."

"Well, you'll have to develop a bit more stamina

then. People are coming and going the whole time. The more you play the more you earn. Come on, forget about being tired, because you've got another half hour to go."

I rolled my shoulders and shook my arms to get the ache out of them, then with an inward sigh I took up my bow again. My eyes briefly met the eyes of the tall man. He gave me a sympathetic smile as though he understood completely how I felt. I smiled back. His cheeks, I noticed, were like a hamster's cheeks, sort of pouchy, and he had a very lined forehead and smiley eyes.

He suddenly got up and came over to me. "Well done. That was excellent," he said warmly as he slipped two pound coins into my palm.

I smiled inanely, said thank you very much and felt like a four-year-old, because I'm never sure how to react when people give me compliments.

"I'd better get on..."

"Don't kill yourself, will you?"

I just smiled again because there was no answer to that.

The next half hour was probably the most exhausting I've ever spent in my life. It's not just the effort of holding the bow and the violin up, it's the tension of being on show and wondering if people like what you're playing, because occasionally I looked round and thought people had irritated expressions on their faces. Maybe I was imagining it, I don't know. I just wished that Hilda Salmon hadn't made me carry on. Whatever she said about customers coming and going, I was sure it was overdoing it to play for so long. After all, most people come into a café to have a quiet chat and a drink or something to eat. All the same several people dropped a coin or two into my case.

When I finally went and sat down with the others, they all gave me tons of compliments, but it didn't make me feel good. I was past feeling anything except exhaustion.

"It's like I've been playing for hours," I replied, rolling my neck and shoulders again to release the tension.

Luce came over at that point. "Puff-Adder wants to see you in the kitchen," she said breathlessly. "And what did that man say to you?"

"He just said he thought I was good, that's all, but I could tell he felt sorry for me, having to play for so long."

"I'm not surprised he thought you were good. How much did he give you?" Fen asked.

"Two pounds."

"Great! How much did you get altogether?" Luce wanted to know.

"I haven't counted it, but it looks like about fifteen or twenty pounds."

"Fifteen or twenty quid! That's excellent,

Lee!" said Andy, clutching my arm excitedly. "You're going to be rich!"

"It means that I won't have to do it again, thank goodness," I told them firmly. "I just don't feel comfortable doing it, and I've played everything I know at least three times. People will get really fed up if they have to listen to that lot again."

"I hope Puff-Adder sees it that way, that's all I can say," Fen remarked ominously.

"Well, if she doesn't, you lay down the law, Lee," said Andy in her usual forthright way. "Don't let her boss you around."

"I'd better go and see her," I said, getting up and heading for the kitchen.

"Very good, Leah. Wasn't so bad now, was it?" were Hilda's first words as I went in.

Kevin turned round briefly but he didn't say a single word, didn't even smile. Perhaps Hilda had put *him* in a bad mood too. All the same it wasn't like Kevin to take his moods out on other people.

"I preferred it when I thought no one was particularly listening," I admitted quietly.

"No point in playing if no one's listening," Hilda replied. Then her eyes took on a very keen look.

"How much did you make?" she asked.

"I'm not sure. Fifteen or twenty pounds, I think."

"Let's have a look then."

"Sorry?" If I sounded surprised it was because I was. Why ever did she want to have a look at the money?

"It's in my case in there," I said, indicating the café with a wave of my hand.

"Don't leave money lying around, Leah. You can't trust anyone these days. Pop and get it," she ordered, as though I was crazy to be standing there when it was perfectly obvious that I ought to be showing her my earnings. I meekly went off and told the girls what I was doing. Andy's face immediately took on a hard look that I know very well.

"Don't you dare let her try to lay claim to any of that money, will you, Leah?"

"She wouldn't, surely?" said Jaimini, a little uncertainly.

Luce followed me into the kitchen this time, so that she could keep an eye on things. Hilda was waiting for me beside the table. I tipped the money out of the case and Hilda shooed Luce away, telling her to attend to the customers, then nimbly counted all the coins into her hand.

"Sixteen pounds twenty-five pence. Very good for a first time – it must be because you're so young. The younger the person, the more generous people are with their money." She did a very short chuckle. "Now, let's see. I reckon two-thirds, one-third is fair."

"Two-thirds, one-third?" My mouth felt dry all of a sudden. I could still hear Andy's voice... *Don't you dare let her try to lay claim to any of that money, will you, Leah?*

Hilda Salmon was beaming at me as though she'd just offered me two free tickets to a pop concert or something. I must have been gawping because she suddenly said, "Well, you didn't think you could make use of the premises and not pay for it, did you? It's not every manageress who'd allow busking, you know. I bet your Jan wouldn't for a start..."

My anxiety obviously showed because she quickly added, "Not that she'd mind me giving my approval, because she was very insistent that I take over the reins completely from her while she's in hospital. 'Just run the place how you think best, Hilda,' were her last words on the subject to me."

Again Kevin turned round and gave us one of those frozen looks of his. I tried a smile but it didn't work and I was glad it didn't because Kevin was not about to give me one back. He just turned round and got on with his cooking.

"So how much...?" I began.

"Well, two-thirds of sixteen pounds is about eleven pounds, and you get five pounds twenty-five. Not bad for an hour's work when you're only thirteen!"

I opened my mouth to protest, because this was even worse than I'd imagined. The two-thirds was going to Hilda and I was to be left with only one-third. I was speechless. The trouble was, she was right. I wouldn't have been allowed to busk if Jan had been there, and though it felt like ten hours, it was true, I'd only been playing for one.

"You'll need to sort yourself out a few more things to play for tomorrow," Hilda told me when she'd taken her share of the money and I was traipsing back into the café.

"Tomorrow! It's my violin lesson."

"Come after your lesson. This is a job, you know. You can't just do it when you feel like it. Believe me, I know about these things. I've had years of experience. Go on, off you go. I'll see you tomorrow."

I was too tired and depressed to argue, so I did as I was told and went.

I must have looked like a ghost when I returned to the others. They hung on to my every word as I reported the conversation, as well as Kevin's contribution.

"She's evil," Luce said, narrowing her eyes and giving us the benefit of her most snakelike eyes.

"I can't see what Kevin's got to be uppity about," Fen said indignantly.

"I expect he feels that maybe Jan wouldn't approve, and so *he* doesn't approve either. Almost as though he's got to kind of represent her in her absence," said Tash thoughtfully.

"I know what you mean," Jaimini agreed softly.

And I knew what Tash meant too. Part of me felt very guilty and bad, and the other part just felt numb. There was none of the feeling of elation that I've had after performing in public before.

Andy hadn't said a word, but she looked like a dormant volcano.

"I'm out of here," she finally said. "Coming?"

"See you tomorrow," Luce said softly.

And we all trooped out, silent and seething.

Mum was not in a good mood when I got in.

"You're spending too much time at that café, Leah. It's got to stop, you know," she fired at me the moment I was inside the door.

It was tempting to tell a lie and say that I'd been at school at an extra practice or something, but I didn't dare in case I got found out, so I just mumbled that I was sorry, and went straight up to my room. Kim followed me and immediately wanted to know how I'd got on. I told her I'd earned five pounds twenty-five.

"Well done!" she said warmly.

"It was really tiring," I added.

"Never mind, at least you did it. That's really great, Leah."

I had intended to keep it a secret from Kim that

Hilda had taken two-thirds of the money, because I didn't want her getting protective of me, and marching in to the café, yelling at Hilda Salmon, or anything like that. But, looking at Kim's smiling face, I suddenly felt the need to confide in her.

"Is it normal to pay the boss at the place where you're busking?" I asked in a small voice.

"Well, usually people busk in streets and in the underground, so I'm not sure." She frowned then said, "I suppose something like ten per cent wouldn't be unreasonable."

"Well, Hilda Salmon took two-thirds of my earnings. I earned sixteen pounds twenty-five altogether."

Kim was speechless for a moment then she shrieked out, "Two-thirds! What a crook! Huh!"

I sat down on the bed and Kim sat down next to me.

"You're stuck, I suppose," she said softly a moment later, all the fight gone out of her. "She's got you, hasn't she? ... What a crook."

When Kim had gone I lay on my bed for ages just thinking about everything until I was sick of it all, so I bounced up and sat at my desk.

"Do something positive," I ordered myself sternly, and I decided to write to Oliver. This would be the letter that would get back at him for Tara. I worked out the craftiest letter I'd ever written in my life. Funnily enough it made me feel better, knowing that I might just give Oliver a touch of the jealousy he'd given me. This is what I wrote:

Dear Oliver,

Thank you for your letter. Well, I finally did it! I plucked up the courage to ask the new manageress of the café if I could busk on the violin in there. To my surprise she said yes. If you met her you'd see why I was surprised. Her name is Hilda Salmon and she's a really strange mixture of strict and lax. Andy doesn't trust her at all and I don't think I do either. She used to run a café in London and she's trying to turn our café into a duplicate of that one. She thought busking was a great idea so I did my first session today.

I earned enough money to buy Dad a really nice present for his birthday. (I decided not to mention that Hilda had taken most of my earnings. I didn't want Oliver to think I was weak.)

I came in for a load of congratulations and praise so I'm quite looking forward to the next time round.

A boy called Pete, who goes to our school and plays the fiddle, said he was very impressed. He's done quite a bit of busking in the past so we were going through some music together to see which pieces were good ones. It's great to have someone showing me the ropes a bit.

Anyway – got to go. I was late back from the café because of going through the music, so now I've got to get on with my homework. See you sometime.

Love, Leah.

Chapter 4

The following morning break at school the six of us got together and made a huge get-well card for Jan. We were all looking forward to her coming back to the café, but I bet I was looking forward to it the most.

"Do you think Puff-Adder will have told Jan about my busking?"

"I doubt it. I bet she knows that Jan would go spare," Andy said.

"It would be terrible if Jan ever found out," I went on, biting my lip.

"Are you going to do it again after your violin lesson today?" Jaimini asked.

"I don't think I've got any choice in the matter," I replied weakly.

We put a lot of effort into our card for Jan, and the finished product looked like something very expensive from a trendy card shop. Jaimini, who's got the best writing and has the best design ideas, wrote *GET WELL SOON JAN, WE ALL MISS YOU LIKE MAD.* Every word had a plate or a knife or a cake or something hanging from it, in a really artistic way. Then we signed our names with loads of kisses.

Fen was going to give it to her mum to give to Jan. We knew from Dee that Jan didn't want any visitors, except Dee herself, that is, because she said she felt too grotty to be sociable even for a short time. Dee did tell us, however, that once Jan was home we could go and visit her.

During the rest of the day my thoughts went between Oliver and Hilda. I couldn't help thinking about my letter winging its way to Oliver. Occasionally I got a pang of remorse and thought that I'd been horrible to mention Pete in the way I did, but then I would start to think about Tara and that would make me feel cross again, and glad that Oliver was about to receive a touch of his own medicine.

When I thought about Hilda I felt mildly sick. I was dreading going into the café, and considered pretending I was ill. The only thing that stopped me from saying I was ill was that the one and only time I'd ever done that in my life, I really had been ill the next day, and I'd had to miss something that I didn't want to miss at all. It was like some sort of punishment for the lie, so I vowed at that time that I'd never do such a thing again.

The dreaded moment finally arrived. The others all got there before me of course, because of my violin lesson, and Jaimini was the one on duty. A quick glance round showed me that there were a few regulars but only two people I'd never seen before. The regulars weren't the same ones who had been there the previous day, though.

It occurred to me for a horrible moment that if they *had* been the same ones who'd been there the previous day, there would be no way they'd want to listen to me playing again. I tried to get this thought out of my head because it was casting another huge shadow over the idea of busking. She – Puff-Adder – seemed to be moving about the café more and more slowly, while Jaimini was flying around like a demented bumble bee. What a cunning woman she is, I thought. She's gradually doing less and less work while we're doing more and more.

"How's Kevin today?" I asked, joining the others. Jaimini was rushing past our table at that moment.

"Not very talkative," was the reply.

"That's nothing new."

"I mean even less than usual," explained Jaimini with an ominous look.

The next minute I was aware of Hilda

approaching. I found myself cringing in my seat as she nudged me and without actually looking at me properly, said, "Get playing then. We've got the sock man coming in a bit, so I want you done by then."

"The sock man!"

"Whoever's the sock man?" we all asked each other when she'd gone.

"I dread to think," answered Fen, putting her head in her hands for a second.

"I suppose I'd better get started then," I said shakily. The feeling that I was doing something wrong was almost unbearable. The only thing that made me get up there and get on with it was the thought of the money, which I desperately needed still.

My first piece today was a very jazzy, modern piece. At least it was supposed to be jazzy and modern, but it came out sounding rather discordant and strange. All the same, Hilda gave a sort of false-sounding cheer, the kind that kids of our age would do, which seemed really strange coming from a middle-aged woman. Then she started tapping her foot in time to the music, only it wasn't quite in time, and it really got on my nerves.

From time to time I made myself look up to see the reactions of the customers. It was very difficult to tell at a glance, and I might have been being hypersensitive, but I definitely thought I detected quite a few looks of irritation on people's faces.

I watched in horror as two regular customers leaned towards each other as though straining to hear what the other one was saying, then made a gesture of I-can't-put-up-with-this-racket, before gulping back their drinks, slapping their money on the table and making a very brisk exit.

During the next twenty minutes or so people came and went but very few people put any coins in my case. I found myself hating being on show like that and praying for the sock man, whoever he was, to come and put me out of my misery.

One of the customers was a blonde girl, who startled me because she looked so much like me except that her hair was much thicker and wavier. She sat down on her own and started staring at me. Even when I wasn't looking at her I knew she was staring at me. I could feel her eyes boring into me. I deliberately didn't look up for ages, but in the end I just had to, and, sure enough, she was still staring; not a nice stare, either.

My eyes went to the door in the hope that I might see the sock man walk in, but no such luck. It occurred to me that if he didn't arrive soon, the place would be closed. I felt too shaky to play any more. Whatever Hilda said, I had to have a break. I went over to join the others and as I did so quite a few people put money in my case.

"Have you spotted the difference, Leah?" Fen asked as I sat down.

I glanced round.

"There's hardly any food being served. It's all drinks."

She was right.

"It's getting very Londonish, this café," Andy put in, with one of her sneers.

"What's with that girl over there?" I hissed quietly, changing the subject.

"I don't know. She can't keep her eyes off you," Luce hissed back.

"She looks amazingly like you, doesn't she?" Fen commented.

"Not really," Luce disagreed calmly.

We all turned to Luce to see if she was joking, because it was plain for anyone to see that the girl looked very much like me.

"Look again," instructed Luce, "and you'll see that apart from the long blonde hair she doesn't look a thing like Leah."

As discreetly as we could, we all took another look, and surprisingly enough, Luce was right.

"There goes Puff-Adder, sizing up the takings," Fen remarked with a disgusted look on her face.

Sure enough, Hilda Salmon was walking past the open violin case, and trying but failing to be subtle about looking in.

"That's enough break, Leah. Come on, the sock man'll be here in a minute."

"Who is the sock man exactly?" Tash asked.

"A great character, Ted. You'll see," chuckled Hilda as she puffed off to the kitchen.

"I suppose I'd better get on with it," I said with a sigh. "Is that girl still looking?"

Fen, who was facing the girl, nodded and said, "She's weird."

I went back to my corner and played again with my usual feeling of total discomfort. None of my playing was any good, because there were too many emotions getting in the way. I made myself keep my eyes down for several minutes, so when I eventually looked up it came as quite a shock to see that the blonde girl had gone.

Only two more people came in during this second session of playing and I realized depressingly that no one had put in any money at all. I knew I was supposed to carry on until the sock man actually arrived, but it was no good, my spirits were at rock bottom and you can't play when you feel like that. No one can.

The moment I'd finished, Hilda appeared in front of me and without a word, rifled through my coins and took out three pounds for herself, leaving me with one pound thirty. Again I was too amazed, exhausted and depressed to protest. I just made my way back limply to the others.

"You're not tough enough," Andy rebuked me when I flopped into one of the chairs at their table. "Don't let her get away with it."

"You're far too soft," Luce agreed, but she wasn't really concentrating on what she was saying. She was staring at the door because the sock man had evidently arrived.

"Wotcha, Ted!" Hilda called out across the café, which made quite a few customers turn their heads.

There was only one table of regulars in there, and I noticed that they rolled their eyes at each other, then one of them got up and paid the bill. It was Jaimini who took the money and gave the change because Hilda was busy helping the sock man to set out his wares on the table that my violin case had just been on.

A few customers immediately got up and went over to look at the socks. I could see them smiling brightly and talking enthusiastically about all the gaudy-looking socks, as they fingered them. They bought five pairs between three of them and seemed very pleased with their purchases.

"I've been trying to work out what's different about this place," Fen suddenly said, which took our attention away from the sock man. "And now I know," she added.

"What?" we all asked.

"The customers. There are just as many of

them but they don't stay for so long, and the regular custom has dropped off."

"Yes, you're right," said Tash thoughtfully as we all looked round.

"Maybe it's just coincidence," Andy said.

"We'll be able to really tell after a few more days," Fen said. Then she stared at the clock on the wall as though she'd seen a ghost. "Omigod, it's ten to six!"

"Ten to six! *Omigod!*" we all agreed, then Fen started gesticulating wildly to Jaimini, whose face took on the same shocked look when she realized what Fen meant. We saw her go straight over to Hilda, and we distinctly heard what Hilda said. "No point in closing when the going's good, is there? You girls aren't exactly flexible, are you?"

Jaimini must have said something about having to go, which we didn't hear, because Hilda's response was, "Just stay till six then. Only ten more minutes."

We waved to Jaimini and mouthed "Good luck", then went off home. Hilda called out to me just before I got out of the door.

"See you tomorrow, Leah. Make sure you're here with plenty of energy."

I didn't answer her snide little remark, just nodded.

That evening, while we were all sitting round the table eating, Mum gave me a lecture.

"You're spending far too much time in that café, Leah. I'm not happy about it. You're down there every single day and you seem to be staying there for longer and longer. I want you home by five o'clock at the very latest if it's not your turn to work."

I didn't say anything – just stared at my shepherd's pie and wondered how I could possibly make it back by five o'clock unless I started playing the second I walked through the door, and persuaded Hilda that three-quarters of an hour was enough, because it would take me a quarter of an hour to get home. I felt so cross and frustrated because I was trapped. I wished for the millionth time that I'd never even heard of the word busk.

"Well?" Mum said.

"Well what?" I asked, not meaning to sound rude.

"Well, have I got your assurance that you'll be here by five in future?"

"Yes, OK," I mumbled.

"Quite right. Five o'clock," said Dad, who often added completely unnecessary little bits to conversations to give the impression that he'd been joining in, and also to show that he quite agreed with Mum. The truth of the matter was that Dad rarely interfered with Mum's organization of family life. He just fitted in.

If you didn't know Dad you'd think he was quite a bumbly scatterbrain sort of person, but he's not really. It's as though he's worked out that there's no need for two people to be saying all the things that one could easily say, so he doesn't waste his breath. But if ever there was a crisis or if ever Mum was in a situation where she didn't know what on earth to do, Dad would step in and sort everything out. He's no fool, Dad. He's different from lots of fathers but I wouldn't change him for anything.

On Friday after school, the café had much the same feel to it as the previous day. Tash was working and I decided to launch straight in and get the dreaded busking over with. Funnily enough the others had all had lectures from their parents about spending too much time at the café, so for once I'd be playing without the comfort of their friendly faces and loud clapping.

At least I'd have Tash around the place. The sock man was there again and my heart sank at the sight of him because maybe this meant that Hilda wouldn't want me to play till later.

"Is it OK if I play straight away today?" I asked her as politely as I could. "Only Mum says I've definitely got to get back home by five unless I'm actually working."

"Well, I don't really want you playing while Ted's got his socks out. For one thing there's not room for both of you, and for another thing people won't buy socks if there's a violin going on at the same time. I know people, I do. I've worked for years in this business, and the two don't go together. Can't you give your mum a ring and say you'll be a little bit late?"

"Well, not really, because she'd only get cross and maybe stop me coming here altogether, except while I'm working, you see."

I could feel myself getting tense because Hilda Salmon obviously hadn't got a clue what parents were like. It was obvious she didn't have any children of her own. All she cared about was making as much money as possible.

"Can you pack them up and bring them out in a bit?" she suddenly called out to Ted, to my great relief.

But at that moment two boys from our year eleven went over to look at the socks, so Ted didn't move a muscle. The boys spent ages looking and feeling and asking about prices, and in the end bought one pair each. As they went back to their places, two girls who looked about seventeen went over to have a look and they spent ages as well, so by the time they'd also bought one pair each, and Ted had very slowly packed the socks away, it was twenty-five past four.

I felt embarrassed to play in front of the year-eleven boys even though they didn't sneer or anything. I think they were quite taken aback to see a year-eight girl playing her violin in the local café. They didn't put any money in my case, but there were several other new faces in the café and a few of them did put money in when I'd finished. Also, to my surprise, I saw the tall thin man with the pouchy cheeks and the lined forehead sitting there again.

It gave me a horrible jolt when I glanced up at the clock after what felt like hardly any time at all. It said nearly ten to five and I realized there was no way I could play for even another minute. I was on the point of telling Hilda this when I noticed that the tall man was talking to her. He had his back to me but I could see Hilda's face tilted to one side as she looked up at him, rather warily I thought. Then she turned abruptly and went into the kitchen.

Returning a moment later, she handed a bit of paper to the man. He took the paper, threw a quick glance in my direction, smiled when he saw that I was looking at him, then went out.

The moment he'd gone I stopped dithering and quickly stuffed the money into my purse without even counting it and packed away my violin as fast as I could.

"Hold on, young lady, you can't pack up after a short session like that, you know," came the voice I was beginning to dislike more and more.

"You're not doing a runner with my money, are you?" She was grinning at me but I didn't like the grin. Her words had the effect of making me blush furiously because I felt so stupid and guilty.

"I can't stay, I'm afraid," I whispered loudly so as not to draw too much attention to our discussion. I was unzipping my purse as I talked, and trying to sort out the money, but my fingers started fumbling and twitching like mad and I dropped several coins on the floor. To make it worse I had to try to remember how much money was already in the purse so that I could work out how much today's earnings had been, as I hadn't even bothered to count it.

Eventually I handed her two pounds twenty-five and said that I thought that was two-thirds, which I did. Her eyebrows knitted together as she gazed at the money in her open palm, then her eyes slowly looked up until they met mine.

"You could do a lot better if you stayed, you know. Look around. There are quite a few people in here now. Plenty of new faces, and young 'uns some of them. They like a bit of music. You ought to think again before rushing off home, you know."

"I've really got to go or Mum'll go spare," I said in almost a pleading voice, trying my best, but failing, to be a bit tougher like Andy said I should.

"Hm," was her only reply. "What time can you

get here tomorrow then?"

"Well, it's actually my turn to work tomorrow," I began, but she interrupted me.

"Never mind that. Get one of the others to do that. Café helpers are two a penny, but there's not many that can play a fiddle like you. I'll expect you at eleven."

"Eleven!"

"Yes. Why not? You can earn a lot on a Saturday, you know."

I had intended to spend the morning catching up with my homework because I was so behind and I knew that I'd be working all afternoon. All the same I didn't want to argue with her because it would only make me later still, so I said, "Yes, all right, eleven o'clock."

She gave me a curt nod then turned round and I rushed to the door. The café was getting on top of me. It wasn't the same bustling, lovely place it used to be. It was full of strangers, people passing through, and it didn't feel right at all. The last person I saw before I closed the door behind me was the girl with the long blonde hair. She stared at me through the window as I made my escape. All the way home the picture of her face stayed in my head.

My heart was going crazy by the time I fell in through the back door. Mum was waiting for me in the kitchen, looking like thunder.

"Leah, I can't believe what I'm seeing. It's twenty past five and I expressly said not a second after five o'clock. I've phoned Andy, Luce, Jaimini and Fen, and they're all at home. I gather Tash is on duty so where have *you* been?"

"The café."

"The café? By yourself?" Her voice had been getting higher the more agitated she got, but she suddenly dropped about an octave and slowly said, "Oh, *I* see. I presume you've got a boyfriend. Is that it? Hm?"

"No, honestly ... I..."

"Yes?"

In the next few seconds my mind played a two-part conversation at about a hundred miles an hour.

Tell the truth ... say you've been busking.

No chance! She'd kill you!

Say you've only done it this once.

Then she'd say, "OK, but don't do it again," which wouldn't help your case for tomorrow, would it?

Say you've been at a practice at school.

Then she'd say, "Why didn't you say that in the first place, instead of saying you'd been at the café?"

Say you've been in detention.

"Actually, Mum, the truth is, I was in detention. It wasn't really my fault, but there were quite a lot of us in the classroom yesterday lunchtime, and some people were drawing all over the blackboard, and some people were playing on computers that they weren't allowed to play on, and Mr Blundell stormed in and gave everyone a detention, because it was impossible for him to see exactly who the troublemakers were."

"Oh, Leah, there's always something," said Mum, looking tired. I think she was actually relieved to find that I hadn't been in the café with a boyfriend, which made me feel a hundred times worse.

I went upstairs and sat on my bed and thought and thought what I should do. With every fibre in my body I wanted to stop busking. I found myself praying that Jan would come back the very next day and everything would go back to normal.

My last thought before I went to sleep that night was about that tall man. What was he doing there in the café? What was he saying to Hilda Salmon? I didn't want my brain to start being active or I knew I'd never get to sleep, so I shut my eyes tight, only to see another picture, this time of the blonde girl. I turned over and curled right up and eventually the picture must have faded from my mind because the next thing I knew it was morning.

I groaned at the thought of the day ahead as I watched the chink of light between my curtains changing shape. The curtains were moving very slightly in the breeze from my open window.

When I was little and I was worrying about things at bedtime, if it was Mum tucking me in, I always used to ask for Dad to come up and see me. Dear old Dad used to go through my worries one at a time, saying things like, "Well, there's no need to worry about losing your way on the outing because the teachers will be keeping an eye on you the whole time." And I would say, "Yes, but what if I go to the loo and when I come out I find that all the others have gone off somewhere?" And he'd say, "Teachers always keep a count of how many pupils they've got, you know." And then when I was still worrying, he'd say, "You won't be worrying about that in the morning. You wait and see. Things never seem so bad in the morning as they do at night time."

And he was nearly always right. I generally found, and still do, that most of my fears and worries dissolved during the night. But I've also noticed that when it's a really big fear, even the night time can't get rid of it. So here I was with the thought of my day at the café looming ahead of me just as largely as it had loomed last night. As soon as it was nine o'clock I phoned Fen and asked her if she could do my duty. I explained that Hilda wanted me to play all afternoon.

"The only trouble is," she said, "that Hilda's just phoned me here and asked me to work this morning."

"This morning! But we never work Saturday mornings!"

"I know, but there's a big problem."

"What?"

"Mark's left too."

I gasped and asked Fen how she found that out.

"Hilda told me. She's trying to get us six to do more and more. I think it's because we're cheaper, and also she knows that we wouldn't dare interfere with her way of running the place."

"I suppose the truth is that she's got us eating out of her hand because she knows very well that none of us will go crying to Jan, because we wouldn't want to be responsible for making her have a relapse, and also we'd never dare to admit about me busking."

"At least Debra's still working there."

"And Kevin."

"Just about."

"What do you mean?"

"Just that it's obvious that Kevin isn't happy."

"If Kevin went, Hilda would be totally stuck."

"You're not kidding. Do you think the time has come for Jan to know about all the changes?"

We were back to square one.

"Why don't you pack in the busking, Leah?"

"I don't know what to say to her. She's acting like it's my job. I wish I'd never started it."

"Well, it's up to you. She can't force you to

busk, you know. Why don't you talk to Andy about it? She'll back you up. After all, it was Andy who mentioned it in the first place."

"Yeah OK, I'll phone her now."

A minute later I was on the phone to Andy. I told her how worried I was about everything, all about Ted, the sock man, the tall man, and the fact that Mark had now left too and how Fen was going to be working this morning.

Andy agreed to do the afternoon for me, and suggested I play for a little while and then we'd approach Hilda together, and tell her I didn't want to do any more busking.

I felt slightly cheered up by Andy's definite plan of action, and I was also glad that Fen would be around with me in the morning.

Chapter 5

By ten to eleven there were lots of people in the café, mainly new faces. Ted was there with his socks and there was also a woman there with a load of umbrellas for sale. Puff-Adder had squashed them both into my corner, and as soon as I walked in I was greeted with, "You're early but you can give Fen a hand."

I went into the kitchen to find Fen making sandwiches. Kevin was also making sandwiches. What on earth was going on? Neither of them was talking and the atmosphere felt troubled.

"Sandwiches?" I said in surprise.

"Hi, Lee." This was from Fen. The others didn't often call me Lee, apart from Andy. I could tell Fen was really relieved to see me, and wondered what it was that had put Kevin in this cold mood.

He tossed the menu over to me and as I opened

it and read the brand-new handwritten page, I understood. Hilda had completely changed the menu. Gone were all the hot dishes, except for soup, and in their place were loads of different sandwiches and cakes.

"She's turned it into a sandwich bar," I said, thoughtfully.

"You've hit the nail on the head," said Kevin.

"Jan won't be very pleased, will she?" I asked, tentatively.

"I doubt it," was Kevin's terse reply.

I wanted to say, "Why do you only doubt it? Why don't you *know* it?" But the sight of Kevin's dark eyes looking darker than ever, and his body all tense and powerful as he pressed down on the knife to cut the sandwiches into triangles, made me falter.

Fen gave me the teeniest look which said, "Don't say anything else. Kevin's not in the mood for conversation." So I asked instead what I could do to help and Kevin said I could wash up if I wanted. As I washed and cleaned and wiped and tidied I went over the brief conversation that we'd just had, in my head, and I think I put my finger on the reason why Kevin didn't sound totally certain that Jan wouldn't be pleased with this new-style café. It was because actually it was doing quite well. There were more customers on balance, yet it wasn't so labour-intensive to run.

"Ready, Leah?" Hilda's sharp voice interrupted my thoughts.

"Yes, all right," I stammered. Fen's eyes said, "Don't be so limp, Leah." Kevin didn't even look up.

The first thing that hit me when I went through to the café with my violin was the noise. One end of the café looked like a market stall. Because Ted and Beryl, the umbrella lady, were talking quite loudly, the people looking at their wares were also talking loudly, which meant that the customers sitting at the tables had to talk even more loudly to make themselves heard.

Hilda pointed to a place at the other end of the café where she wanted me to stand, so over I went. I was aware of the noise level dropping a little and heads turning to see who this girl with the violin was. I felt horribly conspicuous. There were one or two faces I knew, but most of the customers I'd never seen before. Once again there was a distinct lack of regulars from the "old days", as I called the time before Puff-Adder took over.

I took a deep breath and began to play. After the first few seconds, nobody paid much attention. I was pure background music, in fact sometimes I wasn't even that, because the noise around me was so great. I caught Fen's eye and she put her hands over her ears as if to block out all the talking. I gave her a quick smile, then clearly heard a woman say to her partner, "Ah, doesn't she look lovely when she smiles? Let's give her something, shall we?" That made me feel embarrassed because they were only going to give me money because they liked the way I smiled, nothing to do with whether or not I could play the violin.

When I'd finished, quite a few people dropped coins into the violin case, but though there seemed to be a lot of clanking going on, a quick glance told me that it didn't add up to much. There were several five-pence pieces and even two-pence coins. The lady who liked my smile gave me a massive beam and dropped a ten-pence piece in.

I had a break for twenty minutes and noticed that even during this short time the faces in the café had completely changed. Maybe Hilda knew a thing or two after all. She was certainly getting a great many people through the door. Some people had a sandwich or a cake and some just had a drink. Hilda herself swanned about most of the time with a semi-smile on her face while Fen did all the work. She was obviously very pleased with her business.

Thinking along those lines made me think about Jan, so I went into the kitchen to ask Fen how Jan was.

"Mum said she absolutely loved our card and she sends us loads of love."

"Does she know when she'll be back?"

"She thinks she'll be back a week on Monday."

"Only one more week with Puff-Adder then."

"Let's hope."

I went back into the café.

"Hi!" said a familiar voice behind me.

"Oh, hi Kim."

"This came." She handed me a letter with the familiar big scrawly writing on it, then looked round for somewhere to sit, but there wasn't anywhere.

"This place is doing well, isn't it?" she said, looking round. "She must have a magic touch, this ... what's her name?"

"Hilda Salmon."

"Mm. Anyway, I was only just passing. I'll see you later," and off she went with every pair of male eyes in the room following her exit. Kim has that effect on the entire male sex as far as I can make out. I once told her that, and she just laughed and said I was talking rubbish. Another quick look at that handwriting on the envelope made me nip back into the kitchen to read his letter straight away. Kevin didn't even glance up as I went in, so I leaned against the sink and started reading.

* * *

Dear Leah,

Thanks for your letter. I'm really glad you've got yourself a busking job. I knew you ought to. It's great, isn't it – busking? Do you find it a bit boring on the violin though? I found the sax was perfect because I could play jazz as well. It's hard to find the right sort of classical music, I should think.

I've joined a youth club which has started up in our village. I go every Friday at the moment but I'll probably start going on Saturdays as well if I'm not going to the cinema or a party or something. There's a great atmosphere at the youth club because so many people go, so it's a good place for meeting people.

I played pool with this girl called Ellen last week. She actually beat me! I couldn't believe it. I've never been beaten at pool by a girl before. Len – that's her nickname – has been playing since she was really little, and is like the county champion for her age group – under sixteen. It's funny, you'd expect her to be all boyish and everything, but she's not. She's got long wavy black hair, and dresses in really trendy gear. Anyway, I'd better go. Mum's busy preparing for the next lodger. Mrs Right and Tara are leaving today. I'll miss Tara. I got quite used to her being around.

Hope you earn lots of money. See you sometime.

Love, Oliver.

* * *

Oliver's letter made me feel as though I was covered in little prickles. I found myself rubbing my arms to try to get back to normal. I could just imagine that Len girl with her long wavy black hair and really trendy clothes. Practically the whole letter was about her, apart from the bit at the end about Tara. Oliver made me sick, going on about girls all the time.

"Bad news?" asked Kevin, glancing at my angry face.

"Not really," I replied, breaking into a smile with a huge effort.

He looked at me for a moment as if weighing up whether or not to say something, and finally deciding against it.

I thrust the note into my jeans pocket and went back into the café. That was the other change that Hilda had made, by the way. She encouraged us lot to wear jeans, even to serve. She said she was trying to lose the clinical look of the place and get more atmosphere going. She hadn't succeeded in getting more atmosphere, but she'd certainly achieved a different *sort* of atmosphere.

The door seemed to be more often open than it was closed. Some people popped their heads round, had a look, then disappeared. Others came in, had a quick drink, then went. I didn't like the door being open so much. It made the café have a very casual feel to it, like a shop or something.

After lunchtime, which was no busier than any other time of day, Andy turned up and Fen went. I managed to snatch a few minutes with Andy, and told her what it had been like in the morning. I'd made about two pounds eighty-five, so I'd be getting less than a pound for myself, and yet I'd been playing for ages. I would have much rather just have come to work as usual in the afternoon and earned my proper wage.

The afternoon two sessions that I did were even worse, because there were fewer and fewer people, and those who were there had already given me some money the previous day or the day before that, so they weren't about to pay me again.

I tentatively mentioned this to Hilda.

"Do you think people are getting fed up with my violin?" I asked carefully.

"You've got to keep these things ticking over," she replied. "Believe me, I know. You need a bit of this and a bit of that. Then people keep coming through the door to see what's going on, you see."

By the end of the afternoon I was exhausted. Hilda closed early because she said it wasn't worth staying open any more. Kevin had left ages ago and so had the umbrella lady. As Hilda was putting the closed sign up, three young women with toddlers arrived at the door. I recognized two of them. They were old regulars.

"Oh, are you shutting already?" one of them asked.

"No, you can come in if you want," Hilda replied, opening the door but not looking very welcoming.

"We wanted to eat if possible," said another of the women.

"What did you fancy?" Hilda asked.

"Well – something hot…" said the third woman.

"Sorry, no hot food now. Just sandwiches and cakes," Hilda replied.

The women all looked at each other then thanked Hilda but said they'd leave it after all. Hilda didn't look as though she cared one way or the other, but I did. I had the feeling that those women wouldn't come back again, and if they didn't, there would be quite a few others who wouldn't either.

A moment later I was bending down, putting my violin into its case on the floor, when I heard Hilda and Ted talking on the other side of the café. They couldn't see me and didn't realize I could hear every word they were saying.

"What do you think then, Hil?" asked Ted.

"Going well," she answered with a sort of chuckle.

"Certainly getting the punters in," Ted commented. "When's she coming back?"

"Week on Monday, most likely."

"Do you think she'll go along with it?"

"Yeah, once she gets used to the idea, I think she'll be really chuffed. She won't believe I've done it so quickly either."

"She'll take a bit of convincing to get rid of the last two, won't she?"

"I doubt it. She'll soon see that it makes economic sense – just her and me and the girls. Then all I've got to convince her of is that she shouldn't be working full time because she doesn't want to land herself in hospital again. I don't think that'll be a problem. Then, hey presto, we'll be in business, Ted! You'll have a regular place for your socks and things, and I'll have a half share in this manageress job. Come to think of it, I don't reckon we'll even need the girls after a bit. That Leah's good, though. She plays the piano too, apparently. I was thinking I might get a keyboard in. It'd make a nice change from the fiddle."

"You've got that worried look on your face," Ted suddenly said, which made me jump because I thought for one horrible moment that he was talking to me.

"It's just that Kevin," she replied slowly. "He's going to be a tough one to get rid of. I was hoping he'd have gone of his own accord by now, but he's a persistent one, he is. I'm just relying on the fact that when Jan sees that we don't need all those poncy hot dishes, she'll realize that we don't actually need a chef as such. She and I could do it between us."

"You're relying on a lot, you know, Hil. It's only a matter of time before someone or other goes crying to her giving completely the wrong impression, like that know-all Becky you told me about, or that big quiet fellow – what's 'is name? – Mark."

"I don't think I'm relying on a lot. I've often talked with her about it, you know, and she's always loved listening to my stories all about the old place in London. More than once she's turned to me and said, 'It sounds absolutely brilliant, Hilda.' I reckon she'll be tickled pink, especially as it means that she won't have to work flat out like she used to.

"Quite honestly Ted, it's no wonder she collapsed. She used to kill herself running this place. No, it's better all round what I've done. Anyway," she added with a snort of laughter, "Jan stressed that she didn't want to know about the café. She said, 'I'm leaving it in your capable hands, Hilda. I'm just relieved that someone with your experience is ready to drop everything, and willing to take over with no notice.' Those were her very words, as true as I'm standing here, Ted. And another thing, you can bet your bottom dollar that those girls won't risk going sneaking to Jan, because they know only too well that she wouldn't be happy if she knew Leah was playing her fiddle in here."

"Hadn't you better put a stop to the busking then, Hil?"

"Course I will, but not yet. We've got another week of that girl's profits yet, you know!"

I'd been crouching down so long that my left foot had gone to sleep and I knew that any second it would turn to dreadful pins and needles. But my much bigger problem was whether to show myself. When I'd heard Hilda talk in that greedy way about taking my profits I felt like jumping up and being really angry with her. She made me sick. She might have had perfectly good intentions about changing the image of the café to give Jan a nice surprise, but there was absolutely nothing good about her intentions as far as my busking was concerned.

The trouble was, if I popped up now she'd realize I'd heard every word, and this was definitely a private conversation. On the other hand, if I stayed down and she saw me, it would look like a blatant case of eavesdropping. My heart started racing as it always did when I got myself into a state about something.

"Look at this one," Ted suddenly said. "Aromatherapy! What's that when it's at home?" They both chuckled.

Peering carefully through the table I saw that they were facing the wall, looking at notices on the bulletin board. As quietly as I could, and practically limping because of the excruciating pain in my foot, I slipped through to the kitchen. I thought the sound of my hammering heart might attract their attention, I felt so terrified. I was careful not to let the door swing, then once on the other side of it, I leaned against the wall and slid slowly down it with a feeling of sheer relief.

"Leah?" Andy said worriedly. "Are you OK?"

"Let's get going before I have a nervous breakdown," I replied.

"So you don't want to say anything to Hilda about giving up busking then...? I'll back you up if you do, you know, Lee."

"Not now, no. I just want to get out."

"OK, we'd better say bye to Hilda and Ted though."

We poked our heads round the door briefly, then went out of the back door as fast as we could, while I said a million thank yous to fate for stopping Andy from coming out of the kitchen any sooner and blowing my cover.

Walking briskly away from the café with Andy at my side, I realized I'd done it again. I'd meant to make an excuse for Monday, but as usual I'd chickened out, mainly because I was in such a tearing hurry to get away from the place. It also occurred to me that I hadn't handed two-thirds of my earnings over. I expected she'd demand it on Monday.

As we walked on I told Andy about the conversation I'd overheard. She listened in utter amazement and was obviously as confused by it all as I was.

"It sounds as though Hilda really, genuinely thinks she's doing the best for Jan, doesn't it?" said Andy.

"Yes, but ... she's not, is she?"

"I'm not sure. I just can't work that woman out. I mean, on the one hand, maybe we'd be spoiling a nice surprise if we went telling tales to Jan, but on the other hand, maybe Jan ought to know just how much Hilda has manipulated the whole thing to get what she wants."

"All I know is that I'll be glad when she's gone for good and Jan's back in the driving seat. Then it'll be up to her to do what she wants, won't it?"

That evening I read through Oliver's letter again and felt madly jealous once more. I had thought the mention of Pete might have the effect of making Oliver jealous, and take his mind off Tara Features, but I was wrong. He hadn't batted an eyelid about Pete, and now here was another girl in the picture – Len! Huh! I hated her without even meeting her. Right, Oliver! You just wait!

I decided to reply to his letter straight away while my temper was up.

Dear Oliver,

Thanks for your letter. I've only just had time to read it. I've spent the whole day at the café, busking a lot of the time. I've made quite a bit of money now. In fact I've made enough to go and see this newly-formed band called Boyz Elite. They're absolutely mega. You must have heard of them. Pete's brother Martin is in the band so I'm getting my ticket for half price. Kim and her new boyfriend, Ian, who's got a car, are coming along with Pete and me, and we're going to see Martin backstage at the end, and then go off and have a meal somewhere. I can't wait.

Glad you're enjoying the youth club. I used to have a teddy with an ugly face and only one leg, and that was called Len, funnily enough.

Anyway, I'd better go now because I'm supposed to be going to the cinema.

See you sometime.

Love, Leah.

I read through my letter with great satisfaction. I'd invented the whole story of the band. In fact, come to think of it, I'd invented the entire letter. I hesitated before sticking the envelope down because in my heart of hearts I didn't really want to make poor Oliver jealous... Poor Oliver? What was I talking about? Oliver wasn't poor. I hoped he jolly well suffered. It would serve him right for getting too keen on other girls. I would post the letter the following morning and he'd receive it on Monday.

All day Sunday I debated about whether to carry on busking or whether to get all my courage together and make a stand and tell Hilda that I was very sorry but I didn't want to do it any more. There was a part of me that was thinking, if Jan's coming back the following week, why don't I just do it for one more week? After all, I still needed the money, and the damage was already done. Even if I stopped busking from the very next day, Jan would still find out about it.

I'd only just earned enough to pay Luce back and to buy Dad's birthday present. I still owed Tash a bit and I wanted to surprise Oliver with an unexpected visit, then I could see this Len for myself. I'd need some more money for Oliver's birthday present too. One more week's busking would definitely come in handy. Little did I know what was about to happen.

The next day I turned up as usual at four o'clock. Luce was working that day. It was a few days since she'd seen the café and she told me she couldn't believe the change of atmosphere. Ted was there as usual and this time there was a woman I'd never seen before called Min who was selling home-made greetings cards. There were no customers at all and Kevin was nowhere to be seen. Hilda was looking very grumpy.

"Where's Kevin?" Luce asked tentatively.

"Gone home early. Nothing much for him to do."

"Do you want to do my duty?" Luce asked me in a whisper. "There's no point in you playing to no audience, and I know you need the money."

Hilda couldn't possibly have heard what Luce said, but she must have guessed what it was about.

"You stay put, Leah. There could be a roomful of people in no time at all. You never know."

"Has it been slack all day?" asked Luce.

"Well..."

"Slack as slack can be," answered the card lady, Min, with a very sour look on her face.

"Don't listen to moany Min," said Hilda.

The two women obviously knew each other very well and I began to wonder how many more of Hilda's old cronies would be appearing in the café.

After about fifteen minutes a few people started to drift in and Hilda judged it the right moment for me to start playing, so I just did a short session for about ten minutes. No one gave me anything, but worse than that, the girl with the long blonde hair was sitting there in exactly the same place. She didn't stare quite so much this time, but all the same I felt uncomfortable while she was around, so I went into the kitchen to chat to Luce while I was waiting to see if it was worth doing another session.

A few minutes later, when I returned to the café, I saw that the blonde girl had gone and a few other people had arrived. Luce seemed to be doing all the work while Ted, Min and Hilda were sitting down together with a pot of tea for three. I wandered over to my violin and my heart stood still. The bridge which holds the strings in position and keeps them from touching the neck of the violin had been knocked out of place and broken. Two of the strings had been cut in two, and the other two hung limply against the violin.

It's impossible to explain to anyone who isn't a violinist or who doesn't own an instrument, how terrible it was to see my violin in that state. I could have cried and I felt sick when I considered what the repair cost would be. I just stood there staring and shaking. Any minute now I would burst into tears, so I snapped the case shut and took it into the kitchen without Hilda or the others apparently even noticing. Once inside the kitchen I opened the case dramatically in front of Luce. She stared in horror just as I had done.

"Oh Leah, what's happened?"

"Someone's deliberately vandalized my violin.

It's useless. It was such a good one; my most precious possession, in fact."

With those words I did burst into tears, and when Hilda came in a few moments later, that's how she found me, standing there sobbing with Luce's arm around me. Hilda walked straight over, looked at the violin and said, "However did you do that?"

"Leah didn't do it," Luce replied hotly. "Someone did it while she was in the kitchen. It's a very valuable instrument and it's ruined," Luce went on accusingly.

"Does that mean you won't be able to play it for a while, or can you get it repaired in a bit of a hurry?" was Hilda's next charming question.

There's some sort of bubbling spirit inside of me that sits quietly in a weak little pool most of the time, but just occasionally something ignites it and it whooshes up full of red-hot attack. And that's what happened just then.

"Is that all you care about?" I cried loudly through my tears. "My precious violin has been wrecked and you're worried in case I won't be able to earn you a few quid."

"Oh dear, oh dear, hoity-toity," said Hilda. "I didn't know you had it in you. Well, you're quite right to be upset, I'm sure. I'll forgive you for being impolite, but you let me know as soon as possible what the score is on getting it repaired, because if it's no good then I'll have to see what I can do about getting one of those keyboards or electric pianos in. You're lucky to have a place to play in at all at your age, you know."

With that she turned and puffed back out into the café while Luce and I stared at each other open-mouthed.

"She really is something else!" Luce breathed, taking her arm away from my shoulder.

"I'm going home," I answered quietly. "Do you mind, Luce?"

"No, course not. I expect she'll tell me I can go quite soon. Looks like her great idea isn't quite working after all."

I started to go off through the back door but Luce stopped me.

"Who could have done that to your violin, Leah?"

I stopped in my tracks and realized that I'd been so busy mourning for the violin that I'd not given any thought to who could have actually done the damage. A picture of the blonde girl flashed through my mind instantly, though I'd no idea what possible motive she could have had.

"I have my suspicions," I said. "Unfortunately, I'll never be able to prove anything though."

"Who?"

"That girl who the others thought looked like me. She was in here again today. That's the third time. She never smiles, she just stares. For some unknown reason she must have it in for me."

"But someone would have seen her do it, wouldn't they?"

"Not necessarily. Hilda was deep in conversation with Ted and Min when I went out there and there was hardly anyone else in the place apart from that."

"But surely Hilda or one of the others would have noticed if that girl had walked over to your violin?"

"That's true. I'll go and ask them."

"Yeah, I saw her go over there," Ted told me casually a moment later. "I thought she was putting money in."

"Did anyone else go near it?"

"Not that I noticed," replied Ted, looking at the others.

They both shook their heads.

"What would she go and do that for then?" asked Hilda, as though enquiring why someone had closed the lid of the case or something.

"I've no idea," I answered, turning to go.

"Don't forget to let me know what the repair man says," she threw over her shoulder.

"Honestly," I said to Luce in the kitchen, "you'd think she was enquiring about the tumble-drier or something. She's no idea how important this is."

I suddenly realized something awful and clutched Luce's arm. "What am I going to say to Mum?"

"I wouldn't tell her yet if I were you. I mean, it would be very difficult to explain how it happened, wouldn't it? Couldn't you get it to the shop yourself and find out what the damage is?"

"The music shop's quite a few miles away," I replied despondently.

"What about telling your teacher and begging her not to tell your mum?"

"It's a possibility."

"Good luck," Luce said sympathetically, and I went dejectedly out of the door.

Chapter 6

On Tuesday morning I got another letter from Oliver. We never used to write as often as we had been doing lately. I couldn't help feeling pleased to see his big scrawly handwriting on the envelope, though I was quite nervous about what I might read.

Dear Leah,

Thanks for your letter which I got this morning. I've never heard of that group you mentioned and I told quite a few of my friends about it and none of them had ever heard of it either. Len reckons it's probably one of those small "wannabee" bands. There are masses of those around. Len was thinking of being a singer herself, but she's not sure. People keep telling her she ought to be a model because she's got such a good figure. Personally, I think there are tons of things she could do because she's such an excellent all-rounder.

I never thought I'd enjoy going to the youth club but it's really great. Anyway, the reason why I'm writing is because, as you probably know, our family is coming to see yours this weekend, but I'm not sure if I can come or not. The youth club are putting on this big disco on Saturday and I promised ages ago that I'd help with setting it up and all that. It might be quite difficult to get out of that one. So I'll see you if I see you. OK?

Love, Oliver.

My whole body suddenly seemed to weigh a ton. I lay back on the bed and stared at the ceiling. So that was it then. It looked as though Oliver was chucking me and it was pretty obvious who was taking my place. My sadness was far greater than my anger this time. I mean, let's face it: if Oliver didn't even want to see me, there wasn't much point in me being his girlfriend, was there? I lay there imagining Oliver at his youth club disco, dancing every dance with a girl with long wavy black hair. I also felt cross because Mum hadn't even bothered to tell me that Jocelyn and David, Oliver's parents, were coming at the weekend.

Suddenly there was no point in anything any more. I couldn't busk because I didn't have a violin, but even if I *had* had a violin there would have been no point in busking because I wasn't saving up for anything any more. I didn't need the money to go to Oliver's *or* to buy him a birthday present. Birthday... *Birthday!* Omigod! It was Dad's birthday today! I'd bought him a biography about a famous chess player.

I rushed downstairs with my present and my card and gave Dad a big hug.

"I'm a lucky chap," he said with a wink. "Let's see what's in here, shall we?"

He opened the present with great ceremony and an audience of me, Kim and Mum, all smiling and waiting. "Oh, Leah," he said, regarding the book with bright eyes. "This *is* a treat. Thank you very much indeed." I gave him another hug and he showed me what Mum and Kim had given him. Mum's present was a canvas hold-all and Kim's was a set of toiletries and a washbag. We all chatted over breakfast and that was when Mum mentioned casually that Jocelyn and David were coming at the weekend with Oliver. I was just about to correct her and say that Oliver wasn't coming when I realized that he did say he *might* be coming. It wasn't a definite no.

I started to think about my violin and decided that Luce was right, I should speak to Mrs Prentice, my violin teacher, as soon as possible. After breakfast I waited till Mum and Dad were out of earshot then I quickly phoned Mrs Prentice and asked her if I could possibly change my lesson to today instead of Thursday for this week. Mrs Prentice must have thought I was mad because I was talking in scarcely more than a whisper, petrified that Mum might suddenly appear and hear what I was saying. I explained what had happened to my violin, though I didn't tell her where I was at the time when it had happened.

Mrs Prentice agreed that she ought to look at the violin then put it into the music centre to be repaired. She said that though I couldn't have a lesson, I should drop the violin in to her some time after school. So far so good. All I was dreading now was finding out how much it was going to cost, because unless I confessed to Mum and Dad, I'd have to pay for it myself. Goodness knew how!

The others were all very sympathetic at morning break and also totally gobsmacked that anyone could have done such a horrible thing. When I said that I thought it might have been the blonde girl, we all set our minds to puzzling out what possible motive she could have had for doing such an evil thing, but nobody could think of anything at all. The really bad news was that even if the girl was to come into the café today, there was absolutely nothing I could do about it. I could hardly go marching up and accusing her of damaging my violin, could I? She'd just deny it. I wasn't even sure whether I wanted to go to the café that day, but in the end I decided that I'd just pop in before going to Mrs Prentice's, partly because I was curious to see whether or not it was busy or quiet, and also to see whether Kevin was there or not. I didn't have to be scared about busking any more now I'd got no violin.

The other reason we all wanted to go was to support Jaimini, who was on duty and not really looking forward to it. It just wasn't the same any more with people selling things in there and all the regular trade gone. It was as though the regulars had taken the lovely old atmosphere with them – all the warmth and the bustle. Oh, come back, Jan. Please come back soon.

Fen told us that her mum said that Jan had suddenly made a dramatic improvement and was back home, which got us all very excited. We started making plans to go and visit her. Most of our discussion was about how much we should say to her about the changes at the café. We all agreed that it was important to see how well she was, and then we thought we'd play it by ear, and just feed in a bit at a time, and try to gauge how she was taking it, because, let's face it, we had absolutely no idea whether Hilda's mega-transformation would be met with rapture or horror by Jan.

The atmosphere as we went into the café after school was much the same as the previous day.

There was only a handful of people in there. The faithful Ted was there again. He'd added gloves to his sock collection. Big deal. I was sure now that Hilda had made a huge mistake. Cableden was *not* London, and although her great schemes worked for a while, in the long run, they could never go down well in a small place like Cableden.

Jaimini reported immediately that Kevin was not in the kitchen. She'd tentatively asked Hilda about this and been told that Kevin simply hadn't turned up that day. Apparently Hilda had shrugged and shaken her head with a disapproving look on her face as if to say, "You just can't get the staff these days."

"Hasn't Kevin even phoned in?" Fen asked disbelievingly, when Hilda appeared by our table a second later.

"Oh yes, he just said that he didn't think there was any point in his turning up for work because there was nothing for him to do that somebody else couldn't do just as well. The cheek of it! Debra and I have been holding the fort together. I'm quite glad to see you lot, I can tell you. I've been on my own since three o'clock. What about a couple of you giving Jaimini a hand, hm?"

We weren't sure what to say. It was all so casual. Did she mean that we'd be working properly and being paid or what? We looked at one another to gauge each other's reactions and it was then that

I spotted the dreaded object. On top of one of the tables in the corner was a keyboard. I froze and the others followed my horrified gaze.

"What's that?" Luce squeaked.

"A keyboard," replied Hilda. She grinned at me as though confident that I'd be gushing out my grateful thanks any second. "I said I'd get you one, didn't I?"

"I can't play it," I told her in a rush.

"What do you mean you can't play it? It's just like a piano except more buttons."

"It's not. It's nothing like a piano. You need a completely different technique to play a keyboard. The stuff I play on the piano would sound useless on a keyboard. I'm not all that good, honestly."

"You're too modest. That's your trouble."

"No, I'm not, honestly. I can't play it."

How I wished I'd never come to the café! I pleaded with my eyes to the others, and Luce came to the rescue in her usual way, but for once it was just what I needed.

"She's right, actually. She's useless."

Andy started to protest but quickly shut her mouth when I whacked her on the thigh.

"Anyway, I've got to go," I gabbled on. "My violin teacher wants to see my violin."

"I've got to go too," Andy added, then one by one the others all said the same thing.

Hilda didn't look too pleased, but there wasn't anything she could do about it, so she just went back to work muttering under her breath, while we all crashed out of the café door as though there was a fire or something.

Mrs Prentice lived in a big Edwardian house at the top of the High Street, so it wasn't far to go. All the same I felt puffed out when I got there, but I reckoned it was anxiety and not lack of fitness that had made my pulse quicken so much.

When she saw what a state my violin was in, Mrs Prentice looked really shocked and wanted to know exactly how it had happened. I had been hoping that she wouldn't ask this question, but I had already decided that if she did, I'd tell her half the truth, leaving out the fact that I'd left it unattended in the café. I was just waiting for her to ask me where it had happened, and wondering whether I was in for a big telling-off, but all she said was, "You were very lucky, Leah. It could have been stolen, you know."

"I know, and I'll never do it again, don't worry," I said, feeling ashamed of myself.

"I'll give Farley Music Centre a ring. They should be able to do something with it but you may have to wait a week or two, and it could be quite costly."

"Oh ... you see ... I'm going to have to pay for it myself because I daren't tell Mum and Dad about it. They'd be furious. Do you know how much, exactly, it's likely to cost?"

"I'll ring and find out right now if you want."

So she did, and I listened to the one-sided conversation but couldn't get any idea of how bad or otherwise things were from the tone of Mrs Prentice's voice. By the time she put the phone down, I must have looked like a dog begging for food, I was sitting up so straight, waiting to hear the news.

"Good news," she said with a bright smile. "If I take it in tomorrow it'll be ready by next Monday and it'll probably cost forty-five pounds."

"Forty-five pounds!" I gasped. So this was *good* news! Mrs Prentice saw my glum face and quickly explained that she had expected it to take two or three weeks and to cost a little more. Next she gave me a very teacherish look and said, "I should tell your parents if I were you, Leah."

"No, I couldn't possibly..."

"But it wasn't your fault."

"Yes, it was. I shouldn't have left it lying around."

"But surely the headmistress..."

"No, it wasn't at school, you see."

"Ah."

I'd said it, without even meaning to. She gave me another very teacherish look, but fortunately didn't ask me any more questions.

When I got back home I wanted to get in without Mum hearing me, because I didn't want her to notice that I wasn't carrying my violin. She knew I'd gone off with it that morning, and presumably thought like every other time I'd taken it to school, that it was for some orchestral practice or other.

Unfortunately Mum was in the kitchen when I went in through the back door, but I said I was bursting for the loo, and belted straight through the kitchen and upstairs before she had time to notice anything amiss.

The following morning break, the six of us assembled at the bottom of the netball courts, which is our favourite meeting place. I told the others what Mrs Prentice had said, and all of them immediately offered to help me to pay.

"We'll share it," said Luce. "Six into forty-five goes..."

"Seven pounds fifty each," Jaimini prompted her.

"Yeah, seven pounds fifty. I was just going to say that," Luce said indignantly.

"Look, it's really, really sweet of you all, but I couldn't possibly let you lot pay. Don't worry, I'll come up with something." I tried to look optimistic and confident because I knew I'd feel so guilty if I accepted their offer, but inside I was feeling sick.

It was supposed to be my turn to work at the café after school but I was dreading it in case Hilda made me play the keyboard. I knew I'd die of embarrassment because it would sound so stupid in the café. Keyboards just don't go in cafés.

The others felt sorry for me because I was worrying in my usual style, so they all said they'd come along and try to keep the Puff-Adder off me. None of us felt any enthusiasm at all for the café by now. We were just sticking it out as best we could, waiting for Jan to get back, and praying she wouldn't like all the recent changes. We were relieved her first experience of the new-style café was going to be on a Monday morning, so that we wouldn't have to witness her shock, because however confident Hilda was about how pleased Jan was going to be with the transformed café and its brand-new image, we weren't so sure how she would react.

Fen was going to phone Jan that evening and see if it would be all right for us to go and see her the following evening. We had planned to take her flowers and chocolates and once again I was in the embarrassing position of having no money.

At least my duty today would give me some income, and I had decided that I was going to confess to Mum and Dad about the violin bridge, but say that I'd done it myself by mistake. I'd worked out a story that I thought sounded very believable. I was going to say that when I'd been practising in my room I'd put the violin down on my bed to go to the loo and when I'd come back in, I'd tripped over my case and landed with the force of my hand on the bridge, which had broken it. I'd beg them to pay for it, but offer to pay them back in instalments.

Knowing that I'd worked something out made me feel a bit better, and also the fact that Jan would be back soon lightened my spirits. There was only one major downer in my life and that was Oliver; I couldn't stop thinking about him, and however hard I tried, I couldn't get the picture of him and the girl called Len out of my head. Why should Oliver fancy her more than me? It wasn't fair, it really wasn't.

As I was working I went into the café through the back door to the kitchen and the others went in through the front door.

The atmosphere in the kitchen was so dismal. Kevin wasn't there again, and with no Kevin, and no sizzling and steam, the kitchen seemed unfriendly and empty. It also looked very untidy, which made me feel cross, so I leapt into action. Dumping my bag in a corner and putting on an apron, I began clearing things away and wiping surfaces, thinking all the time that it would need a thorough cleaning and tidying before Jan got back or she'd throw a fit. Unfortunately, I'd hardly begun when Hilda came in and told me to come into the café. She went straight back into the café herself, and I trembled to think what she wanted me for.

If the atmosphere in the kitchen was bad, the café itself was much worse. Ted was in his corner, but apart from him and Andy and the others there were only two other customers.

"Isn't it awful?" Fen hissed at me. "I don't suppose Kevin's there, is he?"

"No, he isn't and yes, it is," I whispered back. "I'm just dreading that any second she's going to make me play that keyboard."

"Just say no," Andy instructed me firmly.

"Going to give us a tune then?" came the dreaded voice behind me.

"Say no," mouthed Luce, hitting me with the fiercest look she could muster in the time.

"I can't play the keyboard," I said, straightening up and looking Hilda in the eyes without flinching. I was quite proud of myself at that moment, I can tell you.

"Tell you what, I'll let you keep all the money from Saturday *and* you can keep all the money today, as it's your first time on the keyboard. Now I can't say fairer than that, can I?" she said, giving me one of her famous nudges as though I were another of her best mates.

I hesitated then, because money, or lack of it, was still my biggest problem. Hilda must have seen my hesitation.

"Tell you what, give it a whirl for a few minutes and if you don't like it, you needn't carry on. How about that?"

Once I'd allowed myself to be open to the idea – even such a tiny bit – I found that I couldn't say no.

"All right," I said, and immediately heard Luce let out her breath in an exaggerated sort of frustrated sigh.

"You give in far too easily," Andy remarked as soon as Hilda had gone.

"It's only because of the money," I defended myself.

"OK, we'll let you off," smiled Tash in her usual way. She didn't like any tensions between her friends, and she could probably tell that part of me felt really bad, but on the other hand, however much I hated, with every fibre in my body, the thought of playing the keyboard, I'd be a fool not to do it if I could earn some badly needed money.

In one way I was glad that there was hardly anybody to listen to me, that I could get my act together without looking a fool, and hopefully by the time more people filled the café, I'd be feeling more confident. So I took a deep breath and went over to sit at the keyboard. I glanced over the buttons and levers, then instinctively reached for the pedal with my foot, but of course, unlike the piano, there isn't a pedal on the keyboard. Then I risked a quick look round to see if anybody was watching me.

To my horror, I saw that there was a group of year-nine boys from our school sitting at one of the tables, all smirking behind their menus. It shows what a terrible state I was in. I'd not even noticed those boys coming in. I felt myself blushing bright pink, and my heart seemed to be beating somewhere in the region of my throat. At the other side of the café Hilda folded her arms and gave me one of her encouraging winks. I wanted to die, or at the very least for the floor to open up and for me and the dreaded keyboard to sink quickly out of view.

My fingers trembled as I pressed various buttons and moved a few levers, then cautiously I played the first chord. My head ached and my eyes suddenly couldn't focus properly. This was stage fright like I'd never ever experienced it before.

I'd once had an awful moment when I'd felt sick at a music festival, but I'd never felt this heavy feeling of being physically unable to play. Goodness knows what it must have sounded like, but I somehow plodded on, and tried to produce something resembling a piece of music that I'd recently played on the piano. But it wasn't working. It was all going horribly wrong. I didn't know what on earth to do.

Even without looking, I was aware of all the staring faces, so I couldn't get up and stroll away as though I'd just been trying the keyboard out. I had to stay there and try to make my fingers work, try to produce some decent music. The smirks from the year-nine boys had become sniggers by then.

My head felt as though it had a tumble-drier inside it, and my eyes still weren't focusing properly. Then just when I thought I was going to faint, the door to the café opened, and all my senses were instantly switched on to red alert as a huge shock bolted through my body and I heard myself gasp. Or was it me? Perhaps it was one of the others.

All I knew was that I was looking straight into the eyes of Jan!

Chapter 7

We must have held each other's gaze for at least five seconds, and at the end of the five seconds I realized that the café was totally silent. That was when Jan's eyes left mine and slowly took in the rest of the room.

My friends looked as dumbstruck as I was – wide-eyed and almost scared-looking. Hilda Salmon had gone all red round her neck, I noticed, and her eyes were darting from side to side. Over her face came a sort of demented grin, and it was obvious at that moment that she really *had* wanted to give Jan a lovely surprise. In fact, it was only just dawning on her, that from the look of horrified amazement on Jan's face, that she'd got it all wrong.

Ted's foot-shuffling that he often did when he was bored had come to a sudden stop on Jan's entrance, and he was desperately trying to catch

Hilda's eye. Even the boys in the café, who probably didn't know Jan from Adam, must have been aware that this was a critical moment because of the suddenly charged atmosphere and the shifty looks that were flying silently around.

Jan slowly turned back to the door and for an awful moment I thought she was going to walk out, but a second later she was facing the café again and the expression on her face had changed to one of complete calm. I knew she was far from calm though, and I expect the others did too, because we've come to recognize Jan's moods and all the signs of her changes of mood as well. There was just a hint of tightness about her mouth and a touch of an angry gleam in her eye that told us what was in store.

I got up from the keyboard, and with jelly knees and a pale face I went to join the others at their table. There wasn't a spare chair at the table, but I so badly wanted to be hidden in a crowd away from that dormant volcano that I squeezed in on Andy's chair, and she moved up without a word.

By this time the boys had turned back to their own conversation, though they were still keeping an eye on what was going on. And what was going on was this: Jan was striding through the café and pushing open the kitchen door. She was about to see how untidy Hilda had let it get. Hilda herself was following her meekly in, reminding me for a moment of a naughty child who'd been told by the head teacher to go to his study.

The moment they'd gone, we all turned to each other and began to talk at once in urgent whispers.

"Didn't she look cross?"

"What's she doing here already?"

"She's going to kill Puff-Adder."

"Do you think we should go in?"

"She's going to kill *us*."

"She's going to kill *me*, you mean."

I was the last one to speak, as you may have gathered.

"Why you, Leah? You were only doing as you were told."

"I wasn't tough enough with Hilda. I knew I couldn't perform properly on the keyboard. I was just being greedy."

Nobody argued or agreed with me. We were all just frowning, wondering, worrying.

"What do you think's going to happen?"

"Look! Ssh! Hilda's coming back."

Sure enough Hilda Salmon, whose whole face and neck were bright red, was shuffling over to Ted. He had to lean right over to hear whatever it was she whispered to him, then he rolled his eyes to the ceiling, mumbled something and started to pack up his sock display.

"Do you think we should go in?" Jaimini repeated, but there was no need to answer because Jan appeared in the café and raised an eyebrow at Fen, then jerked her head as if to say, "Come in here, please."

Fen went off without looking back, even though the rest of us kept our eyes on her back. No sooner had she gone through the swing door, than she reappeared and beckoned us all to follow, which we quietly and sombrely did. This was going to be bad. No. This was going to be awful. I could feel it coming.

"Right," said Jan, addressing us all in an ominously quiet voice, as we stood there in a ridiculous row. "Who's going to tell me what's been happening here since I've been away?"

"Um – we were going to come and see you this evening," Fen volunteered in a shaky voice.

"Yes, we were," we all murmured.

"We got you ... something," Luce added helpfully.

"Are you better?" asked Tash in scarcely more than a whisper.

"Not completely, but I'm well enough to be here, and thank goodness I *am* here, before any further damage can be caused. So what's been happening, hm?" She looked from one to another of us.

I felt it was my duty to speak first, as I was the

one who was the most guilty of all.

"I think Hilda wanted to surprise you..."

"Yes, she's achieved that." Jan's flat voice and level stare unnerved me and I found I couldn't speak.

"We've been dying for you to get back," said Luce, who was actually voicing the biggest thing we all felt.

Jan didn't say anything, which in some way gave us the confidence to go on, and once we'd started we couldn't stop. For the next minute or so we bombarded her with all our pent-up emotions. She just stood there as we took turns to pile on the layers of worry we'd all been feeling.

"We don't like Hilda Salmon."

"She's changed everything."

"We didn't know whether you knew or not."

"But we couldn't tell you anyway."

"Because of me. I've been busking on my violin. I knew if I'd asked you, you would have said no, but Hilda said yes, and I badly needed the money ... so I did it..."

"But the Puff-Adder took more than half of Leah's money, and then the sock man came."

"Then the umbrella woman."

"Then the card woman."

"And all the regulars stopped coming bit by bit."

"And all the atmosphere went."

"We hated it."

"But we couldn't tell you because Dee said you didn't want to be bothered. She said that Hilda Salmon was in charge and even if things weren't run in exactly the same way, we weren't to bother you about it."

"We've just been waiting for you to get better."

"We've been dying for you to get back."

And so we'd come full circle. Luce had repeated her opening words and we all fell suddenly silent, and watched Jan in fear and trepidation. Her face had stayed so still as we'd been talking. Only her eyes had darted from one to another of us depending on who was talking.

She sighed deeply and shook her head, then walked over to the kitchen table. Slowly and heavily she sat down on the edge of the table facing away from us. After only a couple of seconds we rushed round to face her again. We were closer this time. And then Fen broke the barrier and went right up to Jan and put her arms round her. She didn't say a word, just stayed there hugging her aunt tightly.

Jan's arms circled Fen and she rested her head on Fen's, while the rest of us drew a little closer and stood there unsure what to do.

"It's all right. Don't worry," Jan finally said as Fen unpeeled herself but stayed close.

Those words were like hearing that we'd all

passed an exam that we'd thought we'd failed. My whole body wanted to dance. The others obviously felt the same, judging from the relieved smiles on their faces.

"It looks as though I chose utterly the wrong person to take over in my absence. I suppose it was all so sudden. Hilda Salmon just seemed like the perfect person. When I collapsed in the café that time and Dee took me home, Hilda must have seen me arrive, because only minutes later she presented herself at my front door, and as soon as she'd got the picture, she was offering to take over. She insisted that I shouldn't worry about a thing. It seemed like the ideal solution especially as I didn't have time to organize anything else.

"Time and time again she'd told me about the café she used to manage in London and what a great time in her life that had been, and I was taken in by her confidence and enthusiasm. She seemed so right for the job. I never dreamt that she'd try to recreate in Cableden something that had worked years ago in London!

"It's my fault. I'd told Dee that I didn't want to know anything about the café. I knew I'd only worry and get frustrated and depressed because I wouldn't be able to sort things out if anything wasn't quite right. On top of that, the doctors and nurses all insisted that the main reason I was ill in the first place was because of stress. They positively applauded my decision to put the café out of my mind and leave it in the capable hands of someone who knew all about running cafés. I thought I was being so sensible… It just shows."

"We didn't even tell *Dee* what was going on because we knew she wouldn't know whether or not she ought to be passing it on to you. And anyway, Leah overheard Hilda talking to Ted, and it was obvious that Hilda thought she was setting up a lovely surprise for you, so that made us even more sure that we'd better just keep quiet and bide our time."

As all this conversation was going on I'd suddenly become aware of something that was puzzling me. What exactly was Jan doing here? Why had she turned up out of the blue earlier than she'd intended? Had someone told her about the café and its transformation, and if it hadn't been Dee, and it certainly hadn't been Hilda, then who was it? I saw Luce's eyebrows go into that thick straight line and the others all wore half-frowns. They must have been going through the same thought process as me.

"How did you…?" Tash began.

"Kevin," answered Jan simply. "He came to see me yesterday. Apparently he was absolutely torn in two, poor Kevin. On the one hand he didn't want to come telling tales if it was going to upset me and make me have a relapse or something, but on the other hand he was very concerned that things had gone too far and that I needed to know about it."

"That's exactly how we felt," Luce said, and we all nodded vigorously.

"Leah," Jan suddenly said, turning to me.

I opened my eyes wider as my heart beat faster. "Yes?"

"I don't think the keyboard is quite your instrument."

I shook my head slowly, adopting the same serious expression as Jan, then as Andy exploded with laughter, I suddenly realized this was the joke of the century, and we all cracked up, including Jan. It was so lovely to see her laughing again. The relief of it all made our laughter louder and heartier than usual, but we soon stopped when the door opened and in came Hilda Salmon.

None of us knew what words had been exchanged between Jan and Hilda, so we watched their two faces like hawks.

"Glad you're all finding something to laugh at," said Hilda, with a sour, pained expression on her face.

"I think it's some sort of hysterical relief," Jan told her calmly, putting into words exactly what I had been feeling.

"Yes," said Fen, standing up straight. "We're

just glad Jan's better and the café won't need *you* any longer."

Tash and I gasped when she said that. It sounded too strong to actually say, even though it was how we felt. I heard Jan take a sharp intake of breath and Hilda looked as though she'd been punched in the stomach. Her face went all pale then very red.

"I'm not sure..." began Jan.

"*We* are!" interrupted Luce. And nobody argued with that, not even Jan.

"I'll be on my way then if..."

So Jan must have told her to leave straight away, I thought.

Hilda was looking at Jan as though waiting for her to change her mind, but Jan stood firm.

"I'll phone you later, Hilda. We'll need to sort a few things out..."

"I'll be off then," Hilda repeated.

I looked down because however much I disliked and distrusted Hilda Salmon, I hated having to witness any adult being humiliated in front of young people like us lot. Across my mind flew a picture of Miss Farrant, my old music teacher who was dying of cancer. She was a good friend of mine, but hadn't always been. Once I'd humiliated her in front of lots of other people. As I watched Hilda leave the café through the kitchen door at the back, I made a resolution to go and visit Miss Farrant as soon as I possibly could.

"What about the customers, Jan?" asked Jaimini a little anxiously, because we'd been in the kitchen for quite a few minutes.

"Don't worry. I told Hilda to get rid of those boys then put the CLOSED sign up. But there's one thing that's really puzzling me..."

"What?" we all asked with great concern.

"Who is the Puff-Adder?"

"Hilda, because she puffs when she walks," explained Luce very seriously, but we didn't stay serious for long, it was such a ridiculous conversation!

"What's going to happen?" I began in my usual worried voice. "I mean ... how are we going to...?"

"We're all going to work hard to get this place back to how it was," Jan answered, understanding immediately what I was getting at.

"Yes!" said Andy and Fen together, punching the air with their fists. The rest of us just grinned, and the grins broadened as the door opened and in walked Kevin. Immediately we all broke into a cheer and Jaimini went and gave him a big kiss, which isn't like Jaimini at all. Of course that made Luce mad with jealousy so she gave him one on the other cheek.

"Come on you lot. Less of this kissing nonsense. Let's get this show on the road," he said, putting on his apron as though this were just another ordinary day.

"Where did you spring from?" asked Luce.

"I came in through the front door for a change," he answered. "But that," he added firmly, "is the last change that I want to experience round here for a very long time!"

"Apart from the change back to normal," Jan corrected him. "I'm actually supposed to be recuperating gently, by the way," she added almost apologetically.

"Well, *we're* all fit as fiddles," Fen answered, "so tell us what to do." And we started there and then.

We got rid of Hilda's menu and wrote out our own. Jan started ordering all sorts of things that we'd run out of and Hilda had never replaced. Kevin took the keyboard out of the café, while Andy and I put the tables back to how they used to be. The others started tidying and cleaning the kitchen, then Kevin started cooking. It was so lovely to feel the atmosphere creeping back in. I had the same feeling that you get when it's a cold day and the sun suddenly comes out.

"It'll take time," Jan kept saying, "but we'll crack it. You wait and see."

The white linen tablecloths covered by large diamond-shaped paper tablecloths replaced the old plastic things that Hilda had put on and we had a thorough clean-up in the café itself, wiping the blackboard outside, cleaning the windows, watering the plants. Jaimini wrote out a large poster which she stuck to the front window. It said RETURN OF THE GOOD OLD MANAGEMENT – WELCOME BACK, JAN GEESON.

Kevin phoned the local paper and arranged for an advert with that sort of wording to go in to the next week's edition. I had phoned Mum and told her the great news about Jan being back and she'd relented for once and forgiven me for being late.

So at five-forty-five, Tash and Andy, Jaimini and I left Luce and Fen vacuuming, polishing and generally enjoying themselves, while Jan chatted to Kevin and helped him with some good home cooking ready for the freezer. What a day! What a relief!

I was dying to tell Mum all about everything as soon as I got home, though of course I wasn't going to mention the busking. As it happened though, I couldn't get a word in edgeways because Mum was bursting with her own news!

"Guess who's just phoned?" she said. Then without giving me time to guess, she went on, "Geoff Cross. You've been spotted, Leah!"

"Geoff Cross? Who's he?" I didn't know what on earth she was on about.

"He's a freelance film director," Mum replied, eyes dancing.

I didn't know what to say, but it was obvious Mum was leading up to something that was really delighting her. She loves telling stories in tiny stages, Mum does. She just gets your interest up a bit, then stops to see what effect her words are having. It can be really irritating if you are dying to know what is going to happen, but just then, although I was curious, I didn't think this phone call was going to be of interest to me.

"He's directing a pop video."

"A pop video!"

"Yes…!"

Her first words come back to me then… *You've been spotted, Leah!*

A weird sensation was coming over me. The reason it was weird was because it was such an odd mixture of sheer terror and amazing excitement. The terror was because it was slowly dawning on me who Geoff Cross was. He must be the tall, thin man from the café. So if he'd contacted Mum, my secret was out. She would know I'd been lying about where I'd been after school and what I'd been doing.

The excitement was because if Geoff Cross was a film director and I'd been spotted, I was going to be a film star. It just couldn't be. I must have misheard. Mum had my total attention now. She must have noticed the way my body had tensed right up.

"He said he thought your violin playing was excellent, and that apparently your looks are perfect for what he's looking for for this pop video!"

Mum clapped both hands on to my shoulders and I searched her eyes for any sign of crossness, but she was all sweetness and light. What on earth had Geoff Cross said to her then? I couldn't ask without giving away where I'd seen him, so I waited again, hoping that Mum would give me a few clues, but she just stood there beaming widely.

"What's the pop video about? I mean what group is it for?"

"Um ... he did mention the name but I hadn't heard of them and I didn't take it in."

"Are they famous?"

"Not *that* famous, I don't think," she answered. "Aren't you pleased, Leah?" she finally said. "I thought you'd be over the moon. *I* was!"

"Yes, I'm just shocked," I answered carefully, and then I decided to go for the six-million-dollar question.

"But how did he get our number?"

"A Mrs Salmon."

"Mrs Salmon!" I gulped, and racked my brain for what to say next, but there was no need. Mum was back in full flow again.

"He was ever so impressed, you know. He said

you looked perfect and you sounded great," she repeated excitedly. Then she suddenly frowned. "Where was it, by the way?"

"Where was what?" I asked a bit faintly.

"Where was it that he saw you? Where were you playing the violin? He didn't actually say. He just said someone called Mrs Salmon had given him this number and I assumed it was one of your teachers."

"Yes … it was … it is, I mean Mrs Salmon, she's one of our teachers."

I knew I was burbling on, but my brain was doing overtime, trying to work out what to say next. How lucky that I'd only ever referred to Hilda Salmon as Hilda.

"I was at school, you see, and Mrs Salmon asked me to play something in the music lesson."

"But I thought Mrs Merle was your music teacher?"

"Yes, she is, only she's away, and Mrs Salmon is taking her place, and she asked me to play. So I did."

"So where does Geoff Cross come into it?"

"Because the window was open and he was coming into school about something else, and he heard me … and then he saw me, you see…"

I was completely pink by then with the exertion of inventing a story on the spot that Mum would find believable.

So far, so good, I thought as she clasped her hands and carried on excitedly.

"It'll be so good for your career, being in a pop video. If you're going to be a professional musician when you're older you need to grasp every opportunity that presents itself to get yourself known. It's a sought-after role, you know, the girl playing the violin in the pop video. There's another girl going for it too, so there'll be competition."

Mum was so rapt about it all, and I was too, of course, but I was also horribly aware that sooner or later we were going to have to discuss the tricky subject of where my violin was. I started frantically composing confessions in my head but it was no good, they all sounded pathetic and I didn't have the energy to cope with Mum's inevitable temper when she knew the truth.

"I haven't heard you practising for a while, Leah. In fact, now I come to think about it, you haven't played a single note to my knowledge since the weekend."

"I'm sure I must have done," I answered rather pathetically, feeling the net drawing in.

Mum shook her head distractedly as though she was still thinking about that.

"Anyway, don't let's waste any more time. Go and do half an hour before we eat. Go on. Off you go."

I stood there glued to the spot.

"Go on," she repeated, with the tiniest hint of suspicion in her voice.

I obeyed her and went upstairs, even though I knew perfectly well that all I was doing was putting off the fateful moment by just a couple of minutes. Once inside my bedroom I thought of a way to put if off even longer. I would play a cassette of some violin music. I'd got two or three recordings of various things to choose from, and I decided on the easiest sounding pieces. My finger was poised over the PLAY button when the phone rang. After two rings it stopped, so Mum had answered it. I pressed PLAY then, and dared to feel the smallest twinge of optimism.

If I could only pull the wool over Mum's eyes and get through this evening, I could go back to Mrs Prentice's and ask if I could possibly borrow a violin (I knew she'd got a least two spare ones in her house), and with any luck Mum wouldn't be able to tell the difference as long as I was upstairs and she was downstairs.

The feeling of relief that this latest reprieve had given me suddenly got totally shattered by Mum flinging open my bedroom door and confronting me with the angriest expression I'd seen on her face for a long time.

"You lied to me, Leah!" she snapped, eyes glinting dangerously.

Chapter 8

I pressed PAUSE and wished for a second that I was pressing a switch which controlled my life. I stood quite still as Mum continued her smouldering speech.

"That was Geoff Cross phoning to say that he thought that for the audition you should play the piece you were playing in the café just before he spoke to you."

I blushed and felt myself beginning to tremble.

"I can't believe it of you, Leah. I just can't." She stared at me stonily as though this might help her be able to believe it more easily.

"Sorry," I whispered.

After another few seconds' staring she said, "I'll speak to you later. Just get on with your practising."

I nodded and started wringing my hands together, praying that she'd go and leave me to it, but she just stood there.

"Come on, then. Haven't you even got it out yet?" Her eyes darted round the room. "Where is it?"

"I … I left it at school."

"You … you *what*?" she shrieked.

"Sorry."

She put her hands on the side of her face as though she was going crazy and was about to scream or something. Then, just when the tension in my room became unbearable, the doorbell rang.

"That'll be him," said Mum, dropping her hands heavily to her sides. "He was phoning on his mobile just then, to ask where we lived so he could drop in the details of the audition."

Mum rushed off to answer the door and I followed her down slowly.

Five minutes later, Mum, Geoff, Kim (who had just arrived) and I were all sitting in our living room. The adults and Kim were drinking tea, and so far nothing had been said about the audition. All the talk had been the usual sort of boring pleasantries that adults make – the weather, our house, the area, etc.

While everyone around me chatted happily, my mind was doing somersaults. One minute I was thinking excitedly about what a fantastic chance I was being offered, then the next my spirits plunged into depression as I realized that I *had* to confess about my violin.

Into my depression came the smallest ray of hope when it crossed my mind that the audition might be a few weeks away, so I'd just have to get through to Monday, then everything would be all right. Unfortunately, I'd have to accept Luce's offer, but it couldn't be helped and I was lucky to have such kind and generous friends. I could pay them back gradually over the next couple of months and make a few sacrifices in the clothing department.

I was so deep in my own thoughts that I hadn't realized that the conversation had switched to the audition and Geoff was saying something to me. Kim kicked me under the table.

"Wake up, Leah," she said, jokingly.

Geoff gave her a friendly smile and my mind did another somersault, thinking frantically, Oh no, he's seen Kim. He's going to change his mind. He's sure to want Kim to do the role. "Will you have time to prepare by Saturday?" Geoff was saying with a searching look in my direction.

"Um," I gulped. "Saturday!"

"Leah, you obviously haven't been listening," said Mum with a light laugh. Little did Geoff Cross know that underneath her laid-back exterior, Mum was really gunning for me, and as soon as he went I was going to be shot.

"Sorry, I was miles away," I said, going a bit pink, and wondering how I could get out of it at this stage in the proceedings, because no matter how hacked off I was about having to miss this brilliant opportunity, there was no way I could go to the audition without a violin, and that was that. I'd have to think of an amazingly good excuse, though.

"All the best artists live in their own little world," Geoff said with another smile. That was a nice way of excusing me for not being able to concentrate on the smallest thing, I thought.

He then started to tell me slowly about the audition, and I got the impression he'd said it all before but I'd been too wrapped up in my own thoughts to notice.

"This gives you all the details," he said, handing me a few sheets of A4 that were stapled together.

"Who's the other girl?" Mum asked as lightly as she could, but it was obvious to me that she regarded the other girl as a great threat. Kim and I exchanged glances. She knew what I was thinking.

"She's also very talented," Geoff said, adopting a more businesslike tone. It was clear that he didn't want to discuss her. "Anyway, we'll just have to see." He closed the topic firmly, leaving Mum a little more anxious than before, I should think.

"Now here," he went on, turning to page two,

"is a brief résumé of what the pop promo's about." He flipped over another couple of pages. "If you could learn these lines for Saturday that would be great. Even if you don't get the main part we can always use you as an extra, because we need a group of young people chatting and laughing together in the pub at the start of the film."

Aha! Here was my excuse. I hate acting. I mean I really do, so all I had to do was to look suitably horrified at the thought of having to say lines.

"Er ... I'm not sure about actually talking," I stammered.

"Of course you are," Mum interrupted firmly.

A flicker of a frown crossed Geoff's face. "It's just a few lines, Leah."

"She'll be fine," Mum assured Geoff with a sort of brisk smile.

"Right, well, I'll be off then," he said. "And I'll look forward to seeing you on Saturday, Leah."

He must have seen my tenseness. "Relax. There's nothing to worry about. You'll see."

I managed a very weak smile, and then he was gone, with Mum bustling behind to see him out. That left me and Kim. I was on the point of whispering to her to come up to my room, so that I could tell her all about the violin saga, then ask her advice. Before I even had the chance to whisper the phone rang. It was Luce. She didn't understand the geography homework and couldn't get hold of Jaimini. I tried explaining, but it didn't work on the phone so we arranged that she would come round.

The first thing I did once Luce and I were safely up in my bedroom was to show her the script and tell her all about Geoff Cross and the audition and everything. During this Mum called out to me to remind me to do some music theory as soon as Luce had got the geography homework. Luce opened the bedroom door and called back to Mum, "I'm just coaching Leah on her lines, Pat. We'll be as quick as we can."

Mum was completely disarmed by Luce's sweet but sensible tone. She knew Luce had the reputation of being a very good actress, so she was probably thinking that Luce was the ideal person to persuade me that the acting bit of the audition wouldn't be any problem.

"Oh, good..." said Mum. "I expect she could do with a bit of help, and you're such a good actress, Lucy."

Luce shut the door.

"That's it," I cried. "Mum's right. You *are* an excellent actress. *You* should be doing this audition, not me!"

"Just two teeny-weeny problems," Luce replied sarcastically. "One: I can't play the violin, and two: I don't look anything like you. I presume that the long blonde hair is a number one requirement. Honestly, Leah, I don't get you. Anyone else would give their right arm to be in your position, to have been actually spotted for a real live part in a pop video."

"It's not that I'm not grateful and all that, it's just that I don't want to let myself get excited about it, because it's a hundred per cent certain that I won't be able to do it because of not having my violin. I'm just going to have to get a grip on myself and go downstairs and tell Mum I refuse to do it because I don't want to say those lines. That's all there is for it."

Luce let out an enormous sigh as though she'd given up on such a hopeless case as me, then when she'd got the geography homework sorted out, she left, and I went reluctantly downstairs.

Mum smiled at me. She'd obviously decided not to tell me off about the busking for the moment, because she didn't want anything to jeopardize the possibility of my doing the audition.

"How did you get on with the lines?"

"Useless."

Her face clouded over, then cleared again almost immediately. "Don't say that, Leah. You're always putting yourself down. I bet you were great."

"No, Mum, I was useless, and I'm very sorry ... but I'm not doing it."

"Not doing what?"

"The audition."

"You can't not do it!" she practically squealed. "You can't just throw away such a wonderful opportunity. You'd be silly to do such a thing."

"Well, I'm sorry, Mum, but it's my decision. It's my life and *you* can't keep dictating what I do and what I *don't* do."

Dad had been sitting reading the book I'd given him for his birthday. He was sitting in what we call "Dad's armchair". He glanced up and said to Mum, "She's got a point there, Pat."

I went over to him and gave him a big impulsive hug. "Thanks, Dad."

It was very unusual indeed for Dad to make such a direct positive statement, especially when it was disagreeing – however gently – with Mum.

Mum was as surprised as I had been. I quickly spoke before she had a chance to come back at Dad. "Anyway, Mum, what about Jocelyn and David? I thought you said they were coming on Saturday?"

"Well, they can still come. They'll just have to come in the afternoon instead. The audition's at ten. We'll be away by ten-thirty, I should think, so we'll be back here by lunchtime."

"But I don't want to, Mum!" I said, raising my voice.

"Mum and I will have a chat about it," Dad said firmly.

Mum opened her mouth to protest but shut it again quickly. It's a funny thing with Mum and Dad. Anybody who didn't really know our family would think that Mum was the one who was in charge because she gives that impression, whereas Dad seems to be the quiet, rather scatty one in the background. But in actual fact, when it comes right down to it, it's Dad who's in charge.

I started to go back upstairs, letting out a sigh of relief because for this evening at least it looked as though I'd managed to get away without having to confess about the violin being broken. I made a mental note to make sure I got home from school before Mum for the next couple of days, so that I could say that I'd already done my practice when she got home.

On Thursday after school my plan worked perfectly. The others went down to the café and I went straight home, even though I would have much preferred to go to the café and see how the transformation back to normal was going. The only reason I wanted to get home was to see if there was a letter from Oliver by any miracle. I was praying that he'd regret saying all that he'd said about Len, and beg me to forgive him. And of course I would forgive him, because despite everything I still wanted to be his girlfriend. I know that's pathetic of me, but I can't help it where Oliver's concerned.

Luce had got the others to try to persuade me to borrow a violin, make a full confession to Mum and go to the audition. Only Andy knew how torn I was, and took my side.

"Look, if Leah doesn't want to do the crummy audition, she doesn't want to do it, and the sooner you lot realize that, the better."

I had smiled gratefully at Andy and thought how lucky I was to have such a strong-minded best friend.

Friday was more difficult than Thursday to get over the violin problem, because Mum was getting pretty insistent on hearing a bit of practice going on. So that's when I resorted to the cassette idea. Only I'd had a brilliant brainwave since the last time. This time I put on a cassette of me practising. Mrs Prentice had always encouraged me to tape my practice from time to time so I could really hear my mistakes when I listened to it. Mum would definitely be taken in this time. I felt horribly deceitful, but kept telling myself it would only be for another two days.

Eventually Saturday morning dawned and I crept around the place very softly so that I wouldn't draw attention to myself. I didn't know if Mum had accepted that I refused to do the audition, or what. I could sense that it would only take the tiniest thing to tip her over the edge and make her pounce on me and drag me screaming and kicking to the audition. What happened next even I couldn't have foreseen.

It was eight-thirty a.m. and Luce suddenly came crashing round to our house. All my great ideas about tiptoeing about the place were completely blown to pieces by Luce entering like a whirlwind, and announcing loudly and clearly that I *had* to go to the audition.

Mum stopped midway between the kitchen and the living room. Kim leaned curiously over the banister. Even Dad looked up from his newspaper, and I stood like a horrified statue as Luce continued in her most vehement voice, "You know that blonde cow?"

"What?" I asked, but it came out like a peculiar squeak because I couldn't believe the language that Luce was using in front of Mum, and anyway, I didn't know what on earth she was talking about.

"The one who broke the bridge of your violin and caused all that damage," she went on, which made me turn white as Mum took a step backwards and Kim came galloping downstairs for a ringside seat.

I shook my head frantically at Luce, but she didn't notice, she was in such a temper, and anyway it was too late. The damage was done.

"I stayed at Jaimini's last night," she bulldozed on, "and during the evening Dom and Carl came over." (Dom and Carl were good friends of Jaimini and Luce, by the way, who went to a private school about twenty minutes away from Cableden.) "Anyway, Dom was telling us about this girl called Melinda who's in the same class as them. He was saying how cocky she was, always assuming everyone thought she was great. Then Dom said that yesterday she'd made up this ridiculous story that no one had believed, about how some big film producer had discovered her and wanted her to be in this pop video.

"Well, you can imagine, when I heard Dom say that, I nearly shot through the roof. 'Has she got long, blonde hair?' I asked him, and he said, 'Yeah, do you know her?' So I told him about you and the café and how we reckon she vandalized your violin, and Dom said..." Here Luce paused and her eyes opened really wide as she spoke very slowly... "Get this Leah... He said, 'Aha, that makes sense of what Martin heard her whispering to one of his friends.'"

"Who's Martin?" asked Kim, who looked as though she was watching an excellent television programme. Mum's face hadn't moved a muscle since Luce's story had begun. She looked as though she was in shock or something. It was impossible to fathom Dad's expression.

"Martin is Dom's friend. Anyway, Martin heard Melinda whisper to her friend that there wasn't anything in the way of her getting this audition because she'd found out who else was supposed to be auditioning, and when this other person had seen Melinda she'd apparently been so overwhelmed by Melinda's good looks that she'd decided not to audition after all because she didn't think she'd have any chance of getting the part."

"The bitch!" I suddenly blurted out.

"Leah!" Mum cried in shocked tones.

Dad's expression didn't change. Actually, I'd shocked myself. I'd never used that word before, but I was suddenly filled with hatred for this girl who had caused me so much trouble.

"Is this all true, Leah? Somebody has deliberately damaged your violin and you've not only kept that fact from us, you've also been blatantly deceiving us? When did this happen? Hm?"

I opened my mouth to speak, but Luce got there before me.

"Excuse me, Pat, I don't want to be rude, but do you mind if I just say something?"

Luce didn't wait for permission to be granted, she just forged on. "It wasn't actually Leah's fault, and the only reason she hasn't told you is because she was so scared of what you'd say."

I saw Dad smiling to himself, but Mum's face was a picture. It was as if she wasn't controlling it properly and it didn't know whether to look cross or sympathetic, so it came out looking plain weird.

"Come on, Leah," Luce went on excitedly. "You've got to do it now. We can't let that b—, that Melinda get away with this, can we?"

"No, we *cannot*," Kim agreed, leaping to the phone decisively. "Is that the music centre?" she asked about ten seconds later. "Have you got a violin that could be hired for the day, please? ...Full size, yes ... yes, great! How much would it be?... Yes, I'll take it... The name's Kim Bryan... Sorry?... Yes, that's my sister... It's ready already! Oh, fantastic! We'll be there in twenty minutes."

"Your violin's ready, Leah!" Kim told me excitedly as she put the phone down and yanked Dad out of his armchair, thrust his car keys from the mantelpiece into his hand and put a hand on his back to propel him to the door. Dear old Dad. He didn't resist. He obviously thought it was a good idea. A minute later as the car revved up then sped away, Mum and I were still facing each other like statues.

"Come on, Lee, we'll need to go over your lines," Luce said.

"I'll get changed," Mum said, looking bemused, as though the events of the morning were taking her over and there was nothing she could do but go with the flow. Before Luce and I had got to my room I heard her on the phone talking to Jocelyn.

"Yet another change of plan, Jocelyn. It turns out that we *are* going to the audition after all. It's a long story, I'll tell you all about it later, but could we go back to plan B? Do you mind coming after lunch?"

In fact, Luce thought my lines were fine, and I felt much better.

"Keep thinking about that awful Melinda, Lee. It makes you say your lines about ten times better. I can't wait to see you beat her."

"Don't say that, Luce. She's probably a brilliant violinist *and* an excellent actress..."

"So are you."

"No, I'm not..."

I didn't finish it off, but my stupid trade mark was showing through. As usual I was worrying because I didn't think there was any way I could compete with someone like Melinda.

At two minutes past ten we piled into the car and rushed to Crossland Productions. There was Mum, Dad, Kim, Luce and me. A receptionist, who was wearing more make-up than I'd ever seen on anyone, personally led us along two corridors, up some stairs and along another corridor into a room like a very small theatre.

We crept in and I instantly froze at the sight of Melinda on the stage, her long blonde hair swaying like a curtain in a breeze as she played a fantastic-sounding piece on her violin. Nobody turned round or even moved a muscle when we walked in, which showed how mesmerized they were by Melinda, and proved just how good she was.

Geoff Cross was sitting with two other men and a woman in the third row of the audience. Then there were three people standing at the back, and they all looked totally rapt.

Luce gave me a nudge to attract my attention. I turned my ashen face to her and she just smiled. I guessed she didn't want to say anything, she was just sizing up how nervous I was on a scale of one to ten, and I'll tell you. If one was completely calm and ten was in a total stew, then I was eleven!

Melinda's last note was quite high and very loud. She whipped her bow through the air and brought it to her side in a flourish, and you could still hear it resounding all round the theatre in the dramatic hush that she'd created with her talent and her presence. I sank down in the nearest seat as the sound of clapping hit the air. It was odd to hear such a thin noise, but even with so few people clapping, their enthusiasm for what they'd just heard was obvious.

"I can't follow that," I whispered to Luce.

"You didn't hear her say her lines. I bet she was useless," Luce hissed back encouragingly.

"You're just as good as that," Kim whispered

into my other ear, leaning forward from the row behind me.

"Am I?" I asked her, turning round to search her eyes.

"Yes, you are," she replied.

But I didn't believe her. It was all turning out just as Melinda had told her friend it would. I was getting frightened away by the force of her very presence.

I raised my eyes slowly to the stage and as I did, my eyes met Melinda's and she froze at the sight of me. I don't think I've ever seen anyone's expression change so rapidly from smiling contentment to utter hate. So much so that Geoff and the other men all turned round to see what could have brought this on.

Geoff jumped up with a friendly smile and strode up to the back when he saw our little hovering party.

"Leah! Great! Good morning, everybody."

Dad and Geoff shook hands and I noticed how relaxed Dad looked. The two men made a bit of light-hearted conversation, then Geoff put his arm out to me as if to say, "Come on then, let's get going."

I got up with trembling knees, took out my violin and followed him down the aisle.

"Go for it!" Luce hissed at my back.

Melinda didn't move at all. I began to think she

was going to stand there in central stage all the time I was auditioning.

"Thank you very much, Melinda."

Still she just stood there as though she owned the stage or something. Then the one woman on the panel got up from her place in the audience, and going on to the stage she put her arm out and steered Melinda away. Shaking all over I went up the steps and stood on the very spot where Melinda had been.

"Take your time, Leah," Geoff said casually. "No hurry at all. Do you want to tune up?"

The lady returned and walked over to the piano at the other side of the stage and played an A. My violin looked so new and lovely with the bridge in one piece and all the strings tight. It took quite a bit of tuning though, because of the new strings.

After a minute or so, just when I was beginning to feel a tiny bit composed, I happened to glance towards the wings to the side of the stage, and there stood Melinda oozing hatred from every pore in her body – at least that's how it felt from the receiving end.

At that moment, the little pool of liquid deep inside me began to boil, and this red-hot anger welling up inside me made me go marching up to Melinda.

"What's your problem?" I asked her, and it didn't seem like the words were coming out of my mouth at all.

"You," she answered in the same voice.

"What have I ever done to you?" I went on, felling surprised at my own courage.

"This was supposed to be *my* role," she spat, "until *you* had to appear on the scene. Geoff wanted *me* to do the part, and believe me he still does. I could tell from his reaction when I played just then. The only reason he's dragged you in is because he thought he ought to try to make it look vaguely like an audition, to satisfy the other judges. But, quite honestly, you'd be doing us all a favour if you just left now, instead of putting yourself through the humiliating process of being turned down."

With that she strode off, tossing her long thick blonde hair over her shoulder as she went.

As though in a dream I moved back to the centre of the stage and raised my eyes slowly to Luce and my family at the back. On all their faces I saw the same expression, a mixture of concern and relief. Nobody could understand what the problem was and why I'd suddenly gone off into the wings like that, but they were certainly relieved to see me back. That was the impression I got, anyway.

"When you're ready, Leah," Geoff repeated, and I gave Kim another quick look as if to say, "Are you sure I'm as good as her?"

Kim smiled and Luce gave me a thumbs-up sign. I raised my bow but dropped it again almost immediately. It was no good. Melinda had succeeded in what she was trying to achieve. She had completely unnerved me, and I couldn't play. I didn't feel like playing. With every fibre in my body I just wanted to walk away and pretend I'd never ever set eyes on Geoff Cross.

"I'm sorry," I said in scarcely more than a whisper, "but I can't do it." Then I made to leave the stage. I'd only got to the top step when I was met by Mum, who must have positively galloped down the aisle to get to me so quickly.

I had the feeling that everybody was holding their breath as Mum guided me back to the spot in the centre of the stage. We both had our backs to the audience and she spoke to me in a soft voice with not a trace of a whine or a moan or even a plea in it.

"I know you think I'm always pushing you into doing things, Leah, and I admit you're right, I'm terrible. So I'm not going to try and persuade you to do this for me, because I promise you it doesn't matter to me one way or the other whether you do it or not. I thought it was important until just now, but now I don't any more."

"Why? What's changed?"

"What's changed is my attitude. And why? Because of that girl we've just seen. I don't want you to get like that – all confident and showy. It's not in your nature. You're not comfortable with it. You're just you, and I wouldn't have you any other way. So if you want to play – and *only* if you want to – play it *your* way. Just be yourself. After all, that's what made Geoff Cross notice you in the first place. 'She's got such a natural quality, has Leah,' were his exact words."

"Is that really what he said?"

"Hand on heart."

She smiled at me and I could feel my confidence flooding back.

"OK, I'll do it," I told her.

"Good girl. And if you get the part, you get it, and if you don't, who cares?"

As soon as she was back in her place I lifted my bow and started to play. I didn't play any of the pieces I'd thought might be suitable. I played a piece that I knew Mum loved and I played it straight from the heart. I didn't move around or do any dramatic flourishes or anything. I just played, but the amazing thing was that for the first time ever, I think, I found myself enjoying playing in public. I was completely relaxed, because it didn't matter whether I got the role or not.

At the end of the piece I lowered my bow and gave my family and Luce a special smile as I walked up the aisle amidst clapping, to join them at the back.

"You've not said the lines," Luce reminded me urgently.

My whole body sighed. I really didn't have the energy or the desire to say the lines. Then, as if on cue, Geoff turned round and called back to us, "We've cut the lines by the way, Leah." And my body sighed again, but with relief this time.

I noticed that one of the other men and the woman were deep in conversation together, and the third man was busy writing.

"Melinda?" called Geoff loudly towards the stage, and she appeared in about two seconds flat, which made me think she couldn't have been far away while I had been playing.

"We'll let you both know," said the man who had been writing. He smiled when he said it, but it wasn't a proper smile. It didn't reach his eyes and it didn't reach anybody else's eyes either. He was definitely not my favourite person.

"Yes, we'll be in touch," Geoff added as though he felt he ought to try and sound a little more enthusiastic.

"When will that be, Geoff?" asked Melinda with another toss of her mane, and a very confident smile.

"Couple of days I should think? … Jeremy?" said Geoff, looking to the other man for confirmation.

"Yes, about that," replied Jeremy with another fake smile.

"Let's get out of here," I said under my breath to Luce.

Chapter 9

When we drew up outside our house, having dropped Luce off on the way, Mum got very excited and loud because Jocelyn and David's car was already there.

"Oh my goodness, they've arrived already," she cried, putting both hands up to her face as though Jocelyn and David were about to catch her without her make-up on or something. "It's only quarter to one, and I said one-thirty!"

"Is it a problem?" asked Dad calmly.

"Well, no, it's just so unexpected," said Mum, who likes to have everything just so and organized. It always throws her when the unexpected happens.

As we got out of the car so did David and Jocelyn. I had been holding my breath from the first moment I'd set eyes on their car, but I could sense a sinking feeling coming over me. I stayed where I was for a moment just to check, but no one got out of the back of their car. The disappointment I felt was almost unbearable. I really thought that if Oliver had appeared at that moment I would have easily forgiven him for Len.

I stared at my violin deep in thought. Dad had paid the forty-five pounds without a murmur, and so far I had got off extremely lightly with the whole thing. I still couldn't believe the way Mum had spoken to me at the audition. There was no doubt that it was that that had made me relax and manage to play. There was also no doubt that Melinda went down about ten times better than I did, but it didn't worry me because Mum was right. It wasn't my style to be all dramatic like she had been, and I couldn't force it.

With a great effort I lugged myself and my violin towards the open front door. The others were all inside, their laughter and chatter pouring out of the door in great gales. When I was almost at the door a voice behind me made me stop in my tracks.

"Hi, Leah."

I turned and felt a great surge of happiness. "Oliver! I didn't think you were coming."

"I changed my mind."

I went towards him but he didn't kiss me. To tell the truth he didn't look all that happy to see me. But I was certainly happy to see him. He looked just as I remembered him, even taller if anything. He hadn't got his earring in, I noticed, but his hair still flopped over his face in a really attractive way.

It suddenly occurred to me that Jocelyn may have forced him to come to Cableden with them, and he really wished he was back home with Len. I felt a stab of jealousy, then I quickly resolved to try not to let it bother me. I'd only got Oliver for a few hours, so I'd better make the most of him.

"Where have you been with your fiddle?" he asked.

"At an audition," I told him, quite proudly because it sounded incredibly cool. "But where did *you* suddenly spring from, Oliver?"

"I went for a walk for something to do while we were waiting for you. Goodness knows why we set off so early."

He followed me into the house and I spent the next couple of minutes thinking that at any moment I might get another surprise, and the lovely Len might suddenly appear.

"How's Len?" I asked, pretending to concentrate on pouring out a can of Coke for Oliver, while the others were all talking loudly around us.

"Oh, OK," he answered rather quickly. "How's Pete?"

"Oh, fine," I answered just as quickly before

Kim could ask who on earth Pete was. I was about to change the subject to the audition, when Oliver turned to Kim.

"How's Ian?" he asked.

Omigod! I'd completely forgotten I'd told Oliver that Kim was going out with someone called Ian.

"Ian?" she said, looking puzzled.

There was nothing for it, I had to do something dramatic, so with a quick swipe of my hand I knocked the glass of Coke over, which caused exactly the right reaction.

"Oh, clumsy me!" I cried, rushing for a cloth while Kim grabbed a wedge of tissues and mopped up the worst of the damage and Mum and Jocelyn fussed around doing nothing, but being very loud about it. As harmony was restored I started talking excitedly.

"The audition was for a pop promo, by the way. I had to play the violin. This guy called Geoff saw me playing and sort of spotted me. He phoned up Mum and said I looked right and I sounded right for the video they were doing."

"What? Saw you busking?" asked Oliver, looking impressed.

"Ssh." I frowned with a jerk of my head in Mum's direction. "Not very pleased," I mouthed.

Oliver grinned and rolled his eyes.

"Are you hungry?" Kim suddenly asked us both.

"Starving," answered Oliver.

"Not really," I replied.

"Well, I'm starving too," she said, ignoring my answer, then she turned to Mum and Dad. "Do you mind if us three go off to the café, Mum? I'll get Danny to meet us there."

Mum looked at Dad who raised his palms as if to say, I can't see anything wrong with that. Meanwhile Oliver looked at me as if to say, "I thought you said Kim wasn't going out with Danny any more." I put a finger to my lips and shook my head very subtly so Kim didn't notice, and fortunately Oliver got the hint, and must have thought that Kim had been through a very hurtful time with her boyfriends and it was best not to talk about it in front of her.

"I've got no money," I whispered to Kim.

"My treat," she whispered back. So off we went.

It was lovely to go in through the front door of the café and find it just as it used to be. The regular customers had started to come in again, the hot food was back on, the original atmosphere was restored, and Jan looked better than I'd seen her for ages.

"Hi," I smiled at her, and she came straight over and chatted for a moment or two before dashing back to her customers.

Mark gave us a quick wave from across the café

where he was making milk shakes, and I zipped across to say "Welcome back" to him. It was all so amazingly back to normal I couldn't believe it. I was burning with curiosity to find out what had passed between Hilda and Jan. Fen had tried to tap her mum for information, knowing that Jan would have confided in her sister, but Dee wasn't giving anything away. She had simply said that it was Jan's business and that if Jan felt like telling us, she would, but meanwhile we shouldn't ask.

The café was practically full and everyone was eating. Becky suddenly appeared from the kitchen and she too gave me a quick wave and nearly dropped the tray she was carrying in the process. I knew that Becky would be changing over with Andy at two-thirty. The others might well turn up too. I felt quite nervous about that because it's not all that easy being with a boy in front of your friends.

Oliver and I ordered pizza and Kim and Danny ordered baked potatoes with curry filling. It felt like a real double date, and everything went wonderfully well for about an hour, then Oliver suddenly remembered the fateful name, Pete.

I glanced at Kim and she gave me a puzzled, questioning look. I then gave her the tiniest shake of my head to say, "Keep out of this," and she immediately got the hint and started talking softly and earnestly to Danny about some television programme they'd both seen during the week.

"When am I going to meet this Pete bloke, then?" asked Oliver, tucking into his pizza.

"Er ... he's away this weekend," I answered, thinking quickly.

"Oh, that's a shame, I was looking forward to meeting him."

"He's nothing special," I said as lightly as I could, which was supposed to make Oliver realize that I preferred him (Oliver) to Pete. Goodness knows whether Oliver got that message or not. He just carried on munching away at his pizza. Then in walked Luce.

"Your mum said you were here. Hi, Oliver!" she said brightly, drawing a chair up and sitting down by me. "Has Leah told you how brilliant she was this morning?"

"Of course I haven't," I butted in, feeling embarrassed.

"Well, she was," Luce summed up as she glanced through the menu which she already knew backwards.

"Mega!" she added.

So then we spent nearly the next ten minutes explaining the saga of Melinda and the violin to Oliver. We had him gripped all the way through, but then as Luce wound up, he suddenly said to me, "And was it Pete who recommended you to play the music you played for the audition?"

"No, I chose that myself," I quickly replied.

"Pete's really nice. You ought to meet him," Luce offered, thinking she was being so helpful to my cause. I had confided in Luce about Andy's great idea of inventing Pete, but none of the others knew about it.

"Yes, I wish I could," answered Oliver, looking vaguely cross.

I felt my whole body tense up, and prayed we'd get off the subject of Pete as quickly as possible. Unfortunately my prayer wasn't answered.

"He may come in soon. He often does on Saturdays, doesn't he, Leah?" Luce blundered on.

"No, he's gone away for the weekend, remember?" I hissed at her with great emphasis on the last word.

"No, he was going to go away, but he told me he'd decided against it because he wanted to hear how you got on in the audition, Leah," Luce ploughed on, even though I was making huge signals with my eyes at her to try and get her to shut up. She obviously thought that the more Oliver heard Pete's name, the more jealous he'd be and the more he'd want to get back together with me. But unfortunately it was becoming very plain to see that all this mention of the name Pete was having quite the opposite effect on Oliver.

There was a brief silence while I racked my brains for something nice and normal to say, but it was Oliver who spoke next with a complete change of subject.

"Can't wait till Tuesday," he began with a sort of secretive look on his face.

It took me a moment to remember what was happening on Tuesday.

"Oh, yes," I babbled, "your birthday. I was going to get your present today actually. We could get it together if you want."

"What were you going to get me?" he asked, which put me on the spot.

"Er – a ring." It was the first thing that came into my head and I regretted it the moment I'd said it. The blood started to rush to my face as I realized that this was far too romantic and over the top. Oh, whatever was Oliver going to think of me?

"Don't get me a ring," he said, digging into his pocket.

The blood drained from my face leaving me feeling pale and weak.

"Look, Len got me this one..."

"Why aren't you wearing it?" demanded Luce, eyeing it aggressively.

"Because it's a bit too small. She's going to get it altered to make it fit."

Leaning backwards in my chair, I realized I felt sick. Kim was still making an excellent job of keeping a separate conversation going between her and Danny, but I could tell she had one ear on our conversation as well. I didn't blame her. No one could fail to be interested in the downfall of Leah Bryan, could they?

I could have killed Luce and I could have hanged, drawn and quartered the luscious Len. I folded my arms and couldn't help the scowl on my face. Oliver turned towards Danny and asked him if he'd watched the United match the previous weekend. Then Oliver and Danny had an animated conversation about football while I sent what-an-idiot-you-really-are messages with my eyes to Luce, and Kim sent what-on-earth's-going-on? messages with her eyes to me!

This was the scene that Andy met when she came over to our table a moment later. She had, of course, come in the kitchen way as it was her turn to work. She smiled round the table and said hello to Oliver, who broke off his conversation as briefly as possible to say hi back to Andy.

Andy's not stupid and it took her no time at all to suss out that there was a huge barrier between Oliver and me, which was making me very unhappy indeed.

With nothing but my best interests at heart, she immediately plunged in with both feet and even outshone Luce in the big booboo of the century stakes!

"Oh, look!" she cried. "There's Pete!"

She was looking through the window at a very tall, very good-looking boy of about sixteen, who I didn't know from Adam, but who was strolling past the café at the time.

Every head at our table whipped round to catch a glimpse of Pete the hero, then my heart missed at least two beats because "Pete" changed his mind about walking past and decided to come into the café!

Andy's eyes turned into two big lumps of coal in her ashen face as she realized her huge mistake. Luce let out one of her nervous giggles, Kim and I gulped, Danny frowned, and Oliver, seemingly oblivious to all this drama around him, watched calmly as Pete went to a table near the counter.

"I'm just going to the loo," mumbled Luce.

"And I must get back to work," stuttered Andy.

"And we're going to choose one of those delicious-looking cakes, aren't we, Danny?" Kim announced to her bewildered boyfriend as she yanked him out of his seat, leaving Oliver and me alone. I was grateful to my sister for being so tactful, even though she must have been very confused.

"Aren't you going to say hello to Pete?" asked Oliver in a strange tone. It was almost sarcastic but with a touch of uncertainty.

There was nothing for it. The game was up. I took a deep breath and opened my mouth to speak, noting that Oliver was staring at me intently. He was obviously relishing the thought of hearing my confession.

"Oh, hi, Leah. I didn't see you."

I looked up into the most amazing pair of dark brown eyes I had ever seen. They belonged to the good-looking boy who'd just come in. Out of the corner of my eye I could see Andy gesticulating at me wildly. She had positioned herself so that *I* could see her, but Oliver couldn't. She was mouthing the word "Pete" while jabbing her finger in the air. Goodness knows how, but she'd obviously somehow managed to persuade this guy to pretend to be Pete.

"Hi, Pete," I managed in a sort of squeak. "Um ... this is Oliver."

Pete, as I'll call him, leaned forwards and shook hands with Oliver, which is something that no one of our age would ever do. I allowed myself a quick glance at Oliver to see how he was coping with the idea of me having this paragon for a good friend. I felt sorry for him for a moment because he looked so shaken.

At that point Kim and Danny returned, and both said hi to Pete. I didn't introduce them because if there really *had* been a Pete he would have already met my sister and her boyfriend.

"How did you get on with the audition?" was Pete's first question. I detected Andy letting out her breath with relief. She'd obviously briefed this poor stranger to ask about the audition.

"Oh, it turned out fine in the end," I began in a rather embarrassed tone. Kim and Luce helped by chipping in from time to time, and between us, the three of us poured out the whole story. Pete looked so genuinely interested that I found him quite easy to talk to after a bit. Luce was positively drooling over him and even Kim looked impressed, which is rare for her. I felt quite sorry for Danny. Presumably Kim had told him at the cake stand that he must go along with the "Pete" thing, but all the same it was perfectly obvious that this good-looking stranger couldn't help his eyes straying over to Kim with her cool magnetic gaze.

I hadn't noticed that Andy had slipped away until she suddenly reappeared and said to Pete, "Sorry to interrupt, but you're wanted on the phone."

He got up and followed her out to the corridor where the phone is. Luce and I talked about an imaginary sister of his while Oliver smouldered beside me and Danny smouldered beside Kim, who was leaning forwards with her elbows on the table, her hands cupped round her chin and an expression of undiluted rapture all over her face.

I began to feel worried. This whole Pete thing was getting out of hand and causing problems that I could never have dreamt possible.

Pete returned a moment later and said, "Sorry, I've got to go. My mum's in hospital and she's asking for me apparently."

Luce and I looked suitably upset, although I was secretly thinking, "Surely you could have come up with something a bit more believable than that!"

"See you on Monday, I expect," he said, looking straight into my eyes. What an actor! He deserved an Oscar! He only spoilt his performance as he turned to go, by saying, "Nice to meet you, Oliver," while his eyes actually said it to Kim.

I noticed she returned his special look with one of her own, and I reckoned Danny noticed too, because his lips tightened.

A moment later Kim and Danny said they were going, and Luce said she ought to be going too. That left Oliver and me, so I ordered more drinks and set about trying to patch things up between us. Half of me wanted to launch into a big confession that Pete didn't exist at all, but then I only had to think about Len and I immediately felt glad that I'd got my own back on Oliver. In fact the more jealous he was, the better.

We talked about things like school and music for a while then I said I was just going to say a quick hello to Kevin because I'd not really seen him since he'd come back to work.

Once in the kitchen I *did* say a quick hello to Kevin, but that hadn't been my reason for going into the kitchen in the first place. I had gone because I wanted to talk to Andy.

"I'm really sorry I landed you in it," she began, "but I hope you were impressed by the way I put my blunder to good use!"

"I feel like a nervous wreck," I told her with a giggle. "What ever did you say to that guy to get him to go along with everything?"

"I just begged him, and he said he'd do it for a laugh, and also because he liked the look of your sister! But listen, Lee, you and Oliver have got to get going double quick. That guy – his name is Ronan by the way – is supposed to be meeting a girl in here. He was too early before, which was why he nearly didn't come in. But the point is, he'll be back with his girlfriend soon. I told him I'd make sure you and Oliver had gone in the next twenty minutes, which gives you –" she looked at her watch – "about four minutes flat!"

Without wasting another second I belted back into the café, but my heart sank at the sight of Jaimini, Fen and Tash sitting at the table with Oliver.

They'd seen me so I couldn't do an about-turn and go back into the kitchen to tell Andy to come and rescue me again. On the other hand Fen and the others would think I was crazy if I started dashing out the moment they'd turned up. I had to think of something, and quickly. I bit my lip as I sat down.

"Congratulations, Leah," they all said warmly. "We've just been hearing about your audition."

"Don't congratulate me. I'll never get the part. That Melinda girl created a far bigger stir than I did. You should have heard her. She was incredible, even though I *do* hate her guts!" I said, sounding extremely normal, considering my heart was banging against my ribs.

I sucked about four mouthfuls of Coke up through my straw, then said, "I wish I hadn't had this Coke. I don't feel like it at all."

"Leave it then," said Oliver sensibly.

Fen, Tash and Jaimini wanted to know all sorts of details about the audition. I answered two or three questions extremely quickly then glanced at my watch and at the door. I was almost having kittens at this stage because at any minute Ronan might walk in with a girl, which could easily blow my whole story.

"We'd better get going, Oliver," I finally said.

"What's the hurry?" he asked.

I couldn't think of a single reason why we should be going, so I just mumbled, "It's OK." And that's precisely when the door opened and in walked Ronan and his girl. His eyes flew open when he saw that we were still there.

Oliver saw me staring at the door as though I'd seen a ghost, and immediately swung round to see what was causing my shock, as did Jaimini, Fen and Tash.

"Hi, you lot," said Ronan, a little falteringly, while the girl beside him looked at him as though he was totally bonkers.

"Um ... this is Jaimini," I began, feeling myself going hot and cold all over, "and this is Fen and Tash." I was just about to add, "This is Pete," when I realized I couldn't, because of the girl at his side, so I stopped abruptly and wished that I could wave a magic wand and disappear into thin air.

I knew Fen and the others were watching me closely. They were presumably wondering how I knew this incredibly good-looking boy, and why I hadn't introduced him.

"This is Leah," Ronan said, turning to his girlfriend and looking totally embarrassed.

"Did your mum change her mind about wanting to see you, Pete?" Oliver asked rather pointedly, and that's when I felt my world come crashing down. I turned my head and waited for the eruption. I didn't know where to put myself. What a feeling! What a ghastly, ghastly feeling! I was quite sure at that moment that being dead would have been a better option than this.

Chapter 10

"Pete?" squealed the girl beside him. "Ronan, you mean!" she added with a nervous-sounding laugh.

Oliver's face took on an expression of suspicion and confusion.

"Ronan?" he said, slowly turning to look at me with a huge question mark in his voice and his eyes.

"I'm going home," I said, standing up with my red face and my knocking knees.

"Are you OK, Leah?" asked Tash, putting a protective hand on my shoulder.

"Not really," I answered, and then I hit rock bottom with the realization that I hadn't even got any money. Kim had paid for all but Oliver's and my drinks at the end. "Can I borrow some money?" I asked Tash very faintly.

"Yes, course," she answered, glancing at the

empty Cokes and putting one pound ten pence on the table. "That enough?"

"Thanks, Tash... Coming, Oliver?"

He stood up dutifully, but probably thought I was a total wombat. The others were looking at us very seriously and sympathetically as though they had just heard some really bad news about us, which I suppose was true in a way.

I was dreading the walk back home, I was in such a strange mental state. It's odd how the mind works, isn't it. Even though things couldn't have been any worse for me at that moment I still felt like laughing. The reason for this was the sight of the people around me. They all had open mouths and wide, staring eyes and I found myself imagining they were trying to catch flies.

"See you on Monday," I managed to utter, which was aimed at Tash and the others.

"Take care," replied Tash in typical sweet, kind Tash fashion. The others said goodbye. Ronan gave me a sort of curt little nod and took his girlfriend's hand as though he was desperate to get to a table where he could get straight down to explaining the whole ridiculous situation that he'd got caught up in. All I could think was how lucky it was that Kim had already gone, or there would have been hell to pay!

Oliver followed me through the door and even walked beside me, but the silence was unbearable, utterly unbearable. Finally, when I could bear it no more, I made a decision. I decided I had nothing to lose as I'd already lost everything anyway.

"I've got something to tell you," I gabbled before I could change my mind. I didn't look at him. Instead I studied my feet as we stood awkwardly in the middle of the pavement.

"That boy in there, you might as well know, isn't Pete at all. Well, obviously you've gathered that… The thing is … I made Pete up. He's a total invention, because I was upset when I read your letter…"

By this time, although I was still looking at my feet, my head was really hanging. Not only did I feel totally stupid because of my miserable confession, but also because now I'd finished it, I didn't know what else to say, and Oliver wasn't saying anything. If any more silence went by I was sure I'd scream.

"What letter?" he asked suddenly.

"Well, the one about Len, of course."

"Yeah, but…"

"But what?"

"Oh, nothing."

We eyed each other warily.

"Anyway, I'm sorry. I know I'm stupid, I just got jealous. There. Now you know exactly what I'm like. I can't help it, but at least I admit it."

I started to walk on but Oliver grabbed my arm and kept his hand firmly on it.

"Look at me, Leah."

I slowly raised my eyes to his. It was the last thing I wanted to do, but he sounded just like a teacher for a moment there, and I obeyed him instinctively.

"You really are a nutcase," he said with a sort of long-suffering but nice smile. I didn't answer because I wasn't sure what he was getting at. "God knows why you got jealous of Len."

"Because you were obviously so taken with her."

"I'm sorry. It wasn't intentional, honestly. It's just that she was a nice girl at the youth club, that's all."

I looked at him and wished I could believe him, but somehow I couldn't.

"But your letter was full of her."

"Well, your letter was full of Pete, let's face it."

"Yes, but that was because of Len."

"But you mentioned Pete before I mentioned Len."

"Did I?"

"Yes."

I frowned as I tried hard to think back. I couldn't have got it wrong. Surely he mentioned Len first. We walked silently for a few minutes, then Oliver suddenly said, "Anyway, let's forget it."

"Forget what?" I asked in a small, scared voice.

"Forget Len and Pete. It doesn't matter about them. We've … we've got each other. That's more important."

My heart started singing, my brain started whirling and my spirits began a crazy dance as I smiled up at him and he took my hand. *He took my hand!*

We didn't let go of hands all the way home. I felt so utterly rapt. We talked about personal things – likes, dislikes, parents and their reactions, friends and their thoughts and habits – real things. It was lovely.

When we were almost home we realized that someone was calling out to us. Turning round, I saw Fen and Tash frantically trying to catch us up.

"We've been calling to you for ages," they puffed as they reached us. Tash noticed straight away that we were holding hands and gave me one of her special understanding Tash smiles. Fen was too full of her news to notice anything.

"Jan's having a party," she told us excitedly, "at the café tonight. Just family and friends…"

"Oh, great! To celebrate the return of the good old place, you mean?"

"Yes. She told me a few things – me and Andy. I went into the kitchen, you see, and she just started talking to Kevin, and then Andy and I got drawn into the conversation."

"What did she say?"

"That she wished Kevin had gone to see her a lot earlier, although she understood why he hadn't."

"Why hadn't he?"

"Because before she went into hospital she spoke to him, on the phone, and told him that Hilda Salmon would be the perfect person for the job because she had loads of experience and was itching to get back into café work. She'd also warned Kevin that Hilda might not manage the place exactly as Jan did, but that he should regard Hilda as the boss all the time Jan was away, as she didn't want to worry about things when she had no control over them."

"In other words Kevin was in exactly the same position as we were."

Fen nodded.

"And did she tell you what she said to Hilda when she came back and saw the wreckage?"

"Not really, she just said that she wanted to scream and bang her fists on the walls and strangle Hilda Salmon, but she truly believed that Hilda thought she was giving her – Jan – a nice surprise, so she used every ounce of self-control she had and just told Hilda that this was *not* what she wanted, and that under the circumstances she felt it would be best all round if Hilda just quietly left."

Throughout all this Fen had me totally gripped.

"So what persuaded Kevin to see Jan in the end?"

"You."

"Me!"

"Yes, he got really worried about you busking. He was worried that Hilda was exploiting you, and he was also worried that busking wasn't the right thing for you to be doing. He said he couldn't explain it really, but when you stood there trembling, but playing bravely away, he felt all protective and anxious about you, yet he knew that really it was none of his business, so he couldn't say anything."

I felt tears pricking the backs of my eyes when Fen said that. Next time I saw Kevin I would thank him. The ridiculous thing was that I would have loved it if he had intervened and announced that he was refusing to allow me to do it any more. That was what I had been crying out for. Maybe Kevin had somehow instinctively known that. He was such a quiet person, Kevin, but more sensitive than anyone would think.

"Will Kevin be there this evening?"

"Yes, of course, we'll all be there."

"Except Puff-Adder."

"Jan says that Hilda's decided to move back to London. She and Ted are going to try and start up some little sandwich bar together. Running our café apparently gave Hilda back her taste for the catering business!"

At that point Fen suddenly stopped talking for long enough to notice that Oliver and I were holding hands. She quickly tried to pretend it was no big deal by saying, "Anyway, the party's at seven o'clock, so see you both later."

We said goodbye, and Oliver and I went into the house. We tried to sidle past the sitting room and go straight up to my room, but unfortunately Jocelyn caught sight of us and called us in.

"Here they are," she said, welcoming us with a big smile and even opening her arms as though we were about three or something.

"How was the café?" asked Mum.

"Brilliant," I replied.

"Because Jan's back?" Dad asked perceptively.

I nodded happily. Everything was brilliant at that moment because I was standing beside the only person I wanted to be standing beside. It was surprising, actually, that no one could see the orange glow around me! I really was on cloud forty-nine!

"I was just telling Pat and Stuart about Tara," Jocelyn went on cheerfully, which made my orange glow fade away and got me off my cloud instantly, leaving a horrid dull memory. I suddenly understood why people talked about being heavy-hearted. My heart felt as though it weighed a ton. And I knew why. Because Jocelyn had presented me with the last piece of the jigsaw puzzle. The reason I'd invented Pete had been because of Tara, not Len at all. I turned accusing eyes on Oliver and waited for him to go red and start stuttering. How could I have forgotten about Tara.

"She was so sweet, wasn't she, Oliver?" gushed Jocelyn.

Go on then, answer that, I thought with a defiant look at Oliver, but for some reason he looked completely calm and normal. I couldn't understand it.

"Yeah, she was really lovely," he agreed warmly. I opened my mouth at the cheek of the boy. How dared he admit it like that!

"And so affectionate," Jocelyn went on.

Oliver smiled as though at the memory, and I sat down quickly before my legs gave way.

"But *you* were her favourite, weren't you, Oliver?" smiled Jocelyn.

He nodded and turned to me enthusiastically. "One time when I took her out, she actually growled at old Mrs Parsons, just because the old lady patted my arm or something. Tara fancied herself as my bodyguard."

This conversation was blowing my mind. Tara growled?

"Why are you looking so totally gormless, Leah?" asked Kim, coming into the room at that moment.

"You mean…" I began, as the fog in my brain cleared and a little rumble of laughter started to form somewhere deep inside me. "You mean, Tara is a dog?"

The others looked at me as though I'd gone mad.

"Course she is," Oliver answered as I began to crack up.

There was a long moment while Oliver looked at me and tried to understand what was amusing me. His eyes narrowed as though he was working on reading my mind, then he too began to crack up.

"Don't tell me you thought Tara was…"

"Your latest girlfriend…" I managed to splutter. By this time I didn't care that Kim and all the adults were tuning in to this ridiculous conversation. They didn't really know what we were talking about anyway, *or* why we were both falling about in hysterics.

"That's why I invented Pete…" I spluttered.

After about five minutes of Oliver and I cracking up every ten seconds or so, the adults began to get slightly exasperated with us and Mum even told me to pull myself together.

I did try to pull myself together, but in the end

it took the mention of the name Len to bring me back to earth. It was Jocelyn who dropped the name in, and this time I noticed Oliver *did* look rather uncomfortable. I hadn't been paying attention to what Jocelyn had been saying just before, but I started concentrating then.

"Such a good youth club," she was saying. "And *such* a shame that Oliver refused to go after the first time."

"Why?" I asked.

"Well, because of that girl Len. He just couldn't stand her at any price. She was always monopolizing the pool table, wasn't she, Oliver? And she was always showing off too. She got on your nerves, didn't she, Oliver?"

"I see," I said, looking Oliver squarely in the face. "So *I'm* a nutcase, am I?"

He blushed and tried to change the conversation. "I still don't see why you thought Tara was a girl and not a dog."

"I'll show you why," I said. "Come up to my room. I've got the letter you wrote, but someone spilt some blue stuff on it in science and so quite a few words were blocked out, and there was nothing left anywhere that said Tara was a dog, so I just put two and two together and made five."

The parents shook their heads as if to say, "Young people today, the messes they get themselves into!" And as Oliver and I went upstairs I could hear Mum lowering her voice and embarking on the tale of the terrible reign of Hilda Salmon.

I showed Oliver the letter and we had another laugh, then he gave me a proper apology for making Len out to be something wonderful when in actual fact he hated her guts. I also made him apologize for not admitting it when I'd done my big admission.

The phone was ringing downstairs as Oliver and I made a pact with each other that from that moment on we'd always be completely honest with each other. Then he got up from the bed and came over to me. I just knew he was about to kiss me, but unfortunately at that precise moment Mum called out for us to go downstairs.

My eyes tried to say to Oliver, "Just ignore her, she's not important. Kiss me, please..."

"Leah! Are you two coming down?" came Mum's unwelcome voice.

"Is there a video camera in here or something?" Oliver asked with a grin.

The spell was broken. I sighed an even bigger sigh and we both went heavily downstairs. As we walked into the sitting room all eyes turned on us. What was going on? Something had changed. It was as though there was magic in the air. I could feel it. I looked round from one person to the next with a question in my eyes.

"You've got it," said Mum. And even then I didn't catch on.

"Got what?"

"Got the part! That was Geoff on the phone."

"I've … I've got it? Unbelievable! Absolutely unbelievable!"

"No, it's not. It's perfectly believable. You were better than her!" Mum said with a big beam. Everyone was beaming, I noticed, and all the beams were identical. Then they all started talking fifteen to the dozen, all except Oliver and me.

"Your mum's right, you know," whispered Oliver, so nobody could hear. "You're the best!"

And then he kissed me.

Also in the Café Club series by Ann Bryant

Have you read?

Go For It, Fen!

Leah Discovers Boys

Luce and the Weird Kid

Jaimini and the Web of Lies

Andy the Prisoner

Tash's Secrets

Fen's Revenge

Look out for:

Luce's Big Mistake

Join

Would you and your friends like to know more about Fen, Tash, Leah, Andy, Jaimini and Luce?

We have produced a special bookmark for you to use in your Café Club books. To get yours free, together with a special newsletter about Fen and her friends, their creator, author Ann Bryant, and advance information about what's coming next in the series, write (enclosing a self-addressed label, please) to:

The Café Club
c/o the Publicity Department
Scholastic Children's Books
Commonwealth House
1-19 New Oxford Street
London WC1A 1NU

We look forward to hearing from you!